Lions
An Imprint of HarperCollins*Publishers*

Illustrated by George Thompson

For Barry with love

First published in Great Britain in 1985
by Dragon Books, reprinted once.
Published in Young Lions in 1988, reprinted twice.
Published in Lions in 1993.

Lions is an imprint of the Children's Division,
part of HarperCollins Publishers Ltd,
77-85 Fulham Palace Road,
Hammersmith, London W6 8JB

ISBN 0 00 673274 7

Printed and bound in Great Britain by
HarperCollins Manufacturing, Glasgow

1

The Phone Call

One peaceful Sunday afternoon in the Stone household, the phone rang.

'I'll get it,' yelled Judy.

A moment later she called, 'Dad, it's for you – it's an American.'

As Dad went to the phone he frowned and said in a puzzled voice, 'But I don't know any Americans,' and then into the phone he said, 'Hello, this is Nicholas Stone speaking.'

Dad spoke for a moment and then said in a whisper, 'It's someone called Malcolm Meilberg. He wants to come and see us.'

Judy's eyes opened wide.

'*Not* Malcolm Meilberg? Not *the* Malcolm Meilberg – the American film producer?'

'I don't know,' said Dad impatiently. 'All I know is he's called Malcolm Meilberg and he wants to drop in.'

'Paul!' shrieked Judy. 'It's Malcolm Meilberg on the phone! He wants to come and see us!'

Paul leapt downstairs, four at a time, and burst into the room.

'Tell him yes, Dad. Malcolm Meilberg, wow!'

'My family will be very pleased to see you, Mr Meilberg. Would later on today suit you?

Good – excellent – see you around five o'clock then.'

'Malcolm Meilberg is coming to tea. Woopee!' yelled Judy. 'Dad, what are we going to give him – we'll have to bake a cake and clean the house and put on our best clothes and hang out a flag and weed the garden and take in the washing and . . .'

'What on earth are you talking about?' growled Dad. 'What's so special about Malcolm Meilberg?'

'Dad, how on earth can you not know about Malcolm Meilberg? He's the most famous film producer in the whole world. He made "Galaxy at War", "Return of the Moody Moon-Monsters", "Whalehunt" and lots of other really great films. He's brilliant, absolutely brilliant!'

'Well, I wonder why he wants to see *us*?' mused Dad.

At that moment Mum came in.

'Malcolm Meilberg phoned, he's coming to tea!' squealed Judy.

'Good gracious!' said Mum. 'Malcolm Meilberg, what a surprise.'

'Isn't it?' said Judy. 'So let's make him a very special cake and clean the whole house up.'

'Now look here, you two,' said Mum. 'If Malcolm Meilberg wants to come to tea that's fine, but he's got to take us as he finds us.'

'But Mum,' said Judy, 'he's very, very famous. We can't just give him an ordinary cup of tea.'

'Why not?' answered Mum. 'And talking about cups of tea, I've been working all morning and I could do with one right now.'

'Sorry, love,' said Dad. 'I'll go and make you one.'

'Honestly,' exclaimed Judy, 'the most famous film producer in the whole wide world is coming round and all you can do is make tea.'

'Exactly,' said Dad. 'And I don't want another word out of you two on the subject until the great man arrives.'

'Well, whatever you say I shall put on my best dress,' announced Judy, sweeping out of the room.

'And I shall put on clean jeans and my "Galaxy at War" T-shirt,' said Paul, and he followed his sister upstairs.

At five o'clock a huge limousine drew up outside the house. Judy and Paul had their noses glued to the window. As they saw Malcolm Meilberg emerge from the car, they raced downstairs to see which one of them could open the door first. Paul wrenched the door open just as Malcolm Meilberg was about to ring the bell. The film producer looked a bit surprised.

'Hi there,' he said. 'You must have been expecting me.'

'We certainly were,' breathed Judy. 'Welcome to London and to Willow Road.'

'We think your films are just fantastic!' said Paul. 'We saw 'Raiders of the Lost Spaceship' four times.'

'I'm very happy to hear that,' replied Malcolm Meilberg. 'Er, can I come in?'

At that moment Dad appeared.

'Good afternoon, I'm Nicholas Stone. You must be Mr Meilberg.'

'That's me, but call me Mal. Delighted to meet you,' the film producer said, shaking hands with Dad. Then he caught sight of Mum.

'You must be Mum,' he said pumping her hand vigorously.

'Well, yes,' she said dubiously, 'I'm Suzanne Stone. Please come in and sit down.'

Soon they were all sitting in the Stones' front room.

'It really is great to meet you folks, I've heard so much about you,' said the film producer with a broad smile.

'Oh?' said Dad, surprised. 'Who from?'

'From Vlad, Vlad the Drac. He talks about you all the time, and speaks very highly of you all.'

Dad groaned. 'Oh no, not Vlad.'

But Judy was delighted.

'You've seen Vlad! How is he?'

'He's fine, just fine – sends his love and is looking forward to seeing you all soon.'

'Where does he think he's going to see us soon?' asked Dad in a suspicious voice.

'Here, in London. He's coming to London to take part in my next film, "Marauding Monsters of the Outer Galaxy".'

'Vlad a film star,' said Judy. 'That's what he always wanted.'

Dad groaned and buried his head in his hands. 'Then I suppose it's in connection with Vlad that you've come to see us.'

'It sure is,' replied Malcolm Meilberg enthusiastically. 'Now Nick, I've come to make you an offer you can't refuse.'

'I wouldn't be too sure about that,' said Dad.

'You haven't heard my offer yet. If you let Vlad stay here while we're making this film, we'll pay you as much money as we would pay a top luxury hotel. Now what do you say?'

'No!' said Dad. 'No, no, no and definitely no!'

'Just a minute,' interrupted Mum. 'It's half my house and I want a say in this.'

'You aren't here every day,' objected Dad. 'You won't be the one who has to put up with him!'

'But Dad,' said Judy, 'Vlad will be out working on the set all day.'

'Sure will,' said Malcolm Meilberg, 'from dawn till dusk.'

'You see?' said Mum. 'And the money will come in very handy. The roof is leaking *and* we need a new car.'

'Well, *I* want Vlad to come and stay,' said Judy. 'I've missed him a lot, and he'd be sad and lonely anywhere else in London.'

'You're all ganging up on me,' groaned Dad. 'Alright Paul, where do you stand on this?'

'Well,' said Paul after a moment, 'it would be fun to be in on a film being made by Malcolm Meilberg, particularly one called "Marauding Monsters of the Outer Galaxy". It sounds great!'

'There you go, Nick,' said Malcolm Meilberg. 'Your whole family want Vlad to come and stay.'

'Wait a minute,' said Dad. 'Not so fast. At the end of the day I'll have to be responsible for that wretched vampire, and I'm not sure I want all the aggro.'

'Come on, Dad!' cried Judy. 'Vlad's not that bad.'

'Not that bad!' exclaimed Dad. 'You've got a short memory, my girl. Remember the disappearances, the police, the rows – no, I can't face it. I can't go through all that again!'

'Nick, come on. Vlad made good in the end. Remember the Great Uncle Ghitza Memorial Fund? A lot of musicians have been helped by that.'

'Oh alright,' said Dad. 'But I'm agreeing under protest and against my better judgement, and only if Vlad agrees to sign a written statement in the presence of witnesses, promising to behave in a reasonable way.'

'I'm sure he'll be happy to do that,' smiled Malcolm Meilberg.

'Right!' said Dad, grabbing a writing pad. 'I'm going to write out my list of conditions right now. Now, let's see – yes:

'*Item 1* He is not to get Vladnapped.

'*Item 2* Under no circumstances is he to vampirise any telephone exchanges.

'*Item 3* He is not to shout at people, particularly not from the window of the house or from the car.

'*Item 4* He is not to say "Poor old Vlad, Poor little Drac . . .'

At this point Judy interrupted. 'That's a bit much, Dad. Surely he can say it now and again?'

'Alright,' said Dad. 'I'll change that to:

'*Item 4* He is not to say "Poor old Vlad, Poor little Drac" more than once a day.

'*Item 5* He is not to fight Mr Punch.

'*Item 6* He is not to go to the swimming pool.

'*Item 7* He is not to swim in my bath.

'*Item 8* He is never to go to the cleaners.

'*Item 9* He is not to even look at a container of tomato ketchup and if he does, I'll chop his head off!

'*Item 10* Finally, he is never, never, never to try and help in any way whatsoever around the house.'

Malcolm Meilberg took the piece of paper. 'If I get Vlad to sign this, can he come and stay?'

'I suppose so,' said Dad gloomily. 'But I'm not happy about it, not happy at all. I predict trouble, nothing but trouble.'

'Oh, come on, Nick,' said Malcolm Meilberg. 'It won't be so bad.'

'It will,' said Dad. 'I know it will. It will be

worse than bad, but as all the others want Vlad to stay I suppose I have to agree. Just don't expect me to be happy about it, that's all.'

'Good!' said Mum. 'Then that's settled. Now we shall drink a little toast to Vlad with our tea. To Vlad the Drac, the Stone family, and "The Marauding Monsters of the Outer Galaxy".'

So they all drank to that and clinked tea cups, laughing – all except Dad, who sat staring into space sunk in deep, deep gloom.

When Vlad was told of the list of conditions he must sign if he was to stay at the Stone household, he made no protest and said he was happy to sign. So three copies of Dad's conditions were drawn up, one for Vlad, one of Dad and one for Malcolm Meilberg. After that the date of Vlad's arrival was arranged and on the appointed day the Stones went to the airport to meet him. They parked the car and went into the airport arrival lounge. On a screen they could see that Vlad's flight from Romania had just flow in.

'I expect Vlad will be a little while,' said Mum. 'It takes time to go through customs and passport control.'

A few people filed past passport control, and then suddenly Vlad flew out. He wheeled right over the head of the man stamping the passports, flew once round the lounge, and then landed on Judy's shoulder.

'Hello,' he yelled. 'Good to see you all. You're looking very well, Judy dear.'

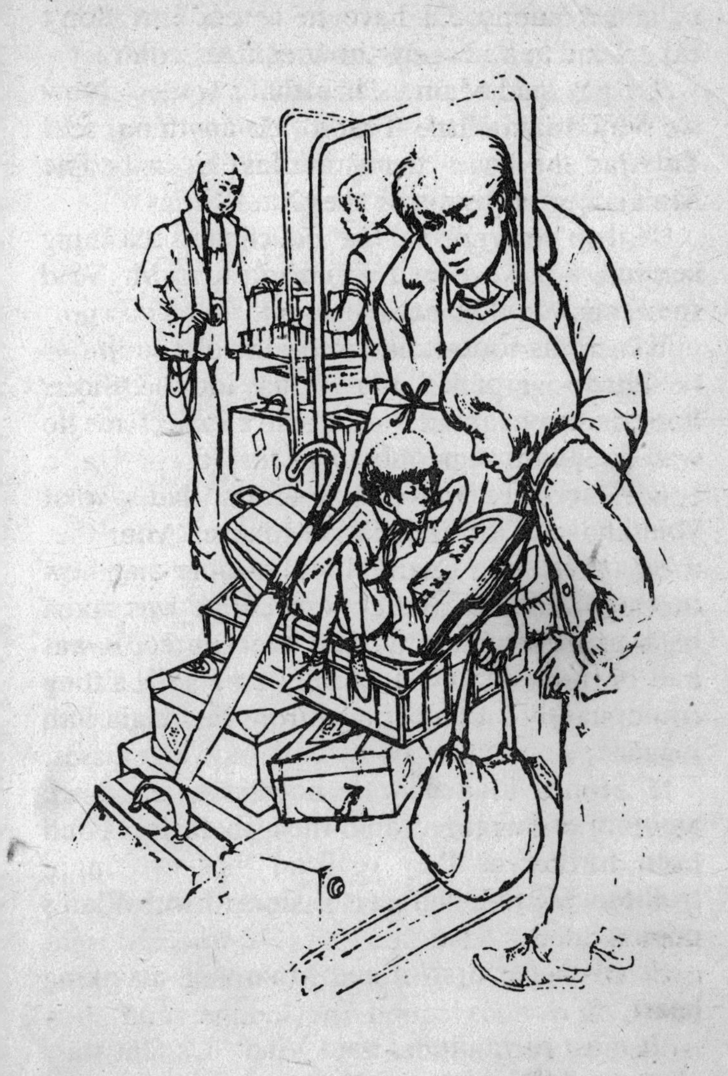
DUTY FREE

At that moment a policeman came up and coughed quietly. Dad groaned. 'Look, it didn't take Vlad ten seconds to break his contract – we've got the law on us already.'

'Why?' said Vlad. 'I didn't do anything, all I did was say hello to my friends. Even people can't object to that, can they?'

'Not to worry,' said the policeman. 'Nothing serious, but we would appreciate it if Mr Vlad the Drac would go back and go through passport and customs control like everyone else.'

'Oh no,' groaned Vlad. 'Just look, Officer, look at those queues. You can't expect me to wait for all those people to go first.'

'I'm sorry, Sir, but I'm afraid that's what you'll have to do, or I'll have to arrest you.'

So, protesting loudly about people and how he should have stayed at home, Vlad was taken back to go through the right procedures. It was half an hour before he finally emerged, sitting triumphantly on top of a trolley piled high with luggage, smiling, waving and blowing kisses. The Stones looked with horror at the huge amount of luggage, and then their faces fell even further as they realized that two more trollies were following, also jammed with Vlad's possessions.

'Is all that yours?' asked Mum with a sinking heart.

'It most certainly is,' said Vlad. 'Us film stars always travel with lots of baggage.'

'Well, there isn't room for most of it in

Willow Road,' said Dad between clenched teeth. 'You'll just have to leave it at the left luggage office.'

'I don't see why,' said Vlad indignantly. 'It could all go in the garage, if you didn't put that silly car in there. There would be plenty of room.'

'Well, I *am* going to put the car in the garage, so you can forget that. Now sort out what you really need and leave the rest here.'

'I'll just take what's on this trolley then,' said Vlad sulkily, 'since you're being so mean. And I'll need my drums.'

'Your *what?'* said Dad faintly.

'My drums. I've taken up playing the drums. It's wonderful – you can make much more noise than on the piano. Crash, bang, boom, boom, boom!'

'No drums!' said Dad firmly. 'Definitely no drums!'

'You didn't mention that on the list of conditions,' growled Vlad. 'I'd never have come if I'd known. I like playing my drums. It's not fair. Poor old Vlad, Poor little Drac.'

'Here we go,' said Dad. 'Now you just remember that you're not allowed to say that again today.'

'Say what?' asked Vlad.

'What it is you're not allowed to say more than once a day.'

'Oh, you mean Poor old Vlad, Poor . . .'

'Quiet, Vlad!' shouted all the Stones.

Vlad glowered at Dad. 'You mean I've really got to stick to all those silly conditions?'

'Yes,' said Dad firmly.

'I can see we're not going to have a nice time,' moaned Vlad.

'Yes, I kind of have that feeling myself,' agreed Dad.

Half an hour later the Stones and Vlad were in their car driving towards Willow Road, with a taxi piled high with Vlad's luggage following them. As they got nearer the house, Dad began to feel more than ever that he had made the wrong decision.

2

Vlad's Birthday

Vlad had arrived in England several days before filming was due to start, to give him time to settle in. But shortly after his arrival Dad got some work, which meant that he was out all day at rehearsals. Mum was busy being a doctor and Paul and Judy were at school. This meant that Vlad was left on his own one day and all the Stones felt it boded no good.

Mum was the first one to get home, and as she put her key in the door she wondered what disaster would have befallen Vlad. Somewhat nervously she called out 'Well, did you have a good day, Vlad?'

'Not bad,' said Vlad.

'What did you do?' asked Mum.

'Well, let me see,' said the vampire. 'First of all the roof caught fire and I called the fire brigade. It's alright, don't look so worried, they put the fire out. Then what happened – yes, that's right, I was having a little sleep when I heard a burglar downstairs but I soon scared *him* away. And then something else happened – Ah yes, the tree in the garden fell down.'

'Just like that?' said Mum.

'Just like that,' said Vlad. Mum went and looked out of the window.

'Which tree, Vlad? They all look alright to me. Oh Vlad, you made it all up, didn't you? There wasn't a fire, or a burglary and no tree blew down. Why did you want to scare me?'

''Cos I'm a vampire,' replied Vlad and clacked his teeth.

'You're not to do it again,' snapped Mum, 'or I'll get very angry!'

'Alright, alright, keep your hair on,' moaned Vlad. 'It's just that I get bored here on my own, and nothing ever happens – Then you come in and talk about your patients and Dad comes in and talks about his rehearsals, and Paul and Judy talk about school, and I don't have anything to talk about, so I made up a few things.'

'I do understand how you feel,' said Mum, 'but you mustn't make up stories. You must learn to tell the truth.'

'Always?' asked Vlad.

'Always,' said Mum firmly.

The next day the family were sitting round the table eating supper.

'You know,' said Mum, 'I said "Good Morning" to Mrs Phillips at number 11 today and she ignored me. I can't understand it.'

'That's odd,' said Dad. 'When I spoke to Pete Mercer next door today, he just went in and slammed the door.'

'It is very strange,' said Mum. 'Two in one day. What can have happened?'

Judy and Paul looked at each other. Vlad licked his fingers in an uninterested way and yawned.

'Vlad,' said Dad suspiciously. 'Have you spoken to either Mrs Phillips or Pete Mercer today?'

'Yes,' said Vlad. 'As a matter of fact I have.'

'With both of them?' asked Dad.

'Yes, both of them,' replied the vampire.

'And what did you talk about?'

'Well,' said Vlad, 'Mrs Phillips said that she thought that you thought she was funny, so I told her that you did and that you called her the fruitbowl on legs because of the awful hats she wears.'

'Oh Vlad, you didn't tell her that?' gasped Mum.

'Yes I did,' insisted Vlad. 'You said to me only yesterday that I was always to tell the truth, so I did.'

'Oh dear,' said Dad faintly. 'And what did you say to Pete Mercer?'

'All I said was – ' replied Vlad, ' – was that you called him Young Frankenstein. He didn't seem to think it was very funny.'

There was a long silence.

'Honestly, Vlad,' said Mum after a few minutes, 'how are we going to live in this street now? None of the neighbours will talk to us.'

'But you said I was always to tell the truth,' Vlad insisted.

'You didn't have to tell lies,' said Paul. 'You could just have kept quiet, talked about the weather and things like that.'

'I can't do anything right,' complained Vlad. 'If

I don't tell the truth it's wrong. If I do tell the truth I'm in trouble. Poor old Vlad . . .'

'Poor little Drac,' chorused the Stones.

'Precisely!' said Vlad.

By the time Monday came Vlad was leaping up and down with excitement.

'I'm tired of hanging about,' he told Judy. 'I want to get down to the serious business of being a star.'

Vlad sat by the window waiting for his big film star's car when the phone rang. It was Malcolm Meilberg to tell Vlad that filming had been postponed for a few days.

'It's all because of some stupid electro-magnetic thingumy-watsit,' Vlad complained to Judy as she brushed her hair before dashing off to school. 'I'll have to be here for another week with nothing to do – Poor old Vlad, Poor little Drac.'

Judy and Paul rushed home that afternoon, expecting to find a disgruntled Vlad, but surprisingly he was chatty and in a good mood.

'Do you know what I just heard on the radio?' he asked.

'How could I possibly know?' said Judy. 'What did you hear on the radio?'

'It said that it is the Queen's official birthday today.'

'Yes, well what about it?'

'What's an official birthday?'

'It's not the Queen's real birthday, it's a day

that has been picked for her birthday to be celebrated on.'

'I thought it was something like that,' said Vlad. 'Do you think she gets presents on her official birthday?'

'I suppose so,' answered Judy. 'Why are you so interested in the Queen's birthday?'

'Because,' said Vlad, 'I don't know when my birthday is, but if I can have an official birthday then I can just choose a day, can't I?'

''Spose so,' said Judy dubiously.

'Well, my official birthday is on Friday,' Vlad announced. 'You can all give me presents.'

When the following Friday came Vlad sat on Judy's shoulder as they went downstairs for supper.

'Do you know what day it is?' asked Vlad.

'What day?' asked Judy, puzzled. 'No. It's not Christmas Day, or Easter or New Year's Day . . .'

'Think again,' said Vlad.

'It's not someone's birthday, is it?' said Judy, thinking hard. 'I know, is it Mum and Dad's wedding anniversary?'

'Not that I know of,' said Vlad huffily. 'It's my official birthday, that's all. It's alright, don't worry, I know what you're thinking – you're thinking it's only Old Vlad – don't worry about him, he's only a silly old vampire.' And he flew back up the stairs.

'Are you coming downstairs for supper?' asked Judy.

'No,' said Vlad. 'No, why bother – nobody loves me, nobody cares!'

'Poor old Vlad, Poor little Drac,' said Judy.

'You may laugh,' said Vlad. 'But it's not a joke when not one single person bothers to remember my birthday.'

'Come and have supper and forget about it,' said Judy. As they went into supper, Vlad carried on a tirade.

'It's a disgrace, that's what it is. Only once a year I ask to be remembered, but no, even that is too much for people. Still, silly me, I ought to have known better. Great Uncle Ghitza told me "Never trust a person" but did I listen – NO – I just went on believing in people. Well, now I know I'm on my own, no one loves me.' And he began to sing loudly, 'Happy Birthday to Me, Happy Birthday to Me, Happy Birthday Poor Old Vlad the Drac, Happy Birthday to Me.'

'Stop that horrible noise out there,' shouted Dad from the kitchen. Paul rushed downstairs and passed Judy and Vlad.

'I'm starving,' said Paul. 'You look pretty miserable, Vlad. What's your problem?'

'People are my problem,' replied Vlad. 'People in general and you in particular.'

'Me!' exclaimed Paul. 'What have I done?'

'It's not what you've done, it's what you *haven't* done.'

Mum stuck her head around the kitchen door.

'Supper's ready, but I don't want Vlad eating with us if he's having a sulk.'

'I hate everyone!' announced Vlad and buried his head in his hands. 'I don't want to see anyone,' he declared.

'You can look now, Vlad,' said Mum.

'Look at what?' moaned the vampire. 'There's nothing worth my while looking at,' and he cast a despairing glance round the room. Then his eyes lit up.

'You didn't forget,' he gasped as he saw a huge cake with lots of candles and 'Happy Official Birthday, Vlad' written on it.

'Of course we didn't forget,' said Dad. 'We just wanted to give you a surprise.'

'Here, Vlad,' said Mum. 'Here are your presents.'

'Cor,' said Vlad, his eyes opening wide. 'Are they all for me? Cor, it's better than Christmas. Then everyone else gets presents too.'

Vlad was thrilled with all his presents. When he had opened them they had a specially delicious supper. Afterwards Paul lit Vlad's candles. 'You've got to blow them all out, Vlad,' Paul told him.

'How many are there?' asked Vlad.

'I'm not sure,' said Dad. 'We weren't sure how old you were.'

'Neither am I,' said Vlad. 'Can I fly over the cake and blow the candles out with my wings?'

'I don't see why not,' said Mum. 'And don't forget to wish.'

'Wish what?' asked Vlad.

'Wish for whatever you want most.'

So Vlad flew over his cake while the Stones sang:

> 'Happy Birthday to you,
> Happy Birthday to you,
> Happy birthday, Dear Vlad the Drac,
> Happy Official Birthday to you.'

'Thank you, thank you,' said Vlad. 'It's been a lovely official birthday. Can I have another one tomorrow?'

'No!'

'No!'

'No!'

'No!' chorused the Stones.

'Alright,' agreed Vlad. 'Who wants a slice of my cake?'

'Well, er . . . it's not a cake,' explained Mum. 'It's a huge tin of furniture polish. I emptied it out of the tin and stuck candles on it.'

'I see,' said Vlad. 'Then you don't want any?'

'No thanks,' said the Stones.

'Not even a little bit?' asked Vlad.

'Not even a little bit.'

'Have it your own way,' said Vlad and enthusiastically tucked into the polish.

'What did you wish, Vlad?' asked Judy.

'Not telling,' said Vlad.

'Oh, go on,' said Paul.

'No!' said Vlad. 'It's a very special vampire wish and I'll vampirise you if you ask again!'

3

Boris the Bat

Judy was sitting quietly watching TV on Sunday afternoon when the door opened and Vlad walked in backwards, dragging a huge parcel behind him.

'What's that, Vlad?' asked Judy.

'It's the script of "Marauding Monsters of the Outer Galaxy",' gasped Vlad, panting.

'What are you doing with it?' enquired Judy.

Vlad dropped the script. 'I am trying to bring it over to you so you can go through it with me, and if you could give me a hand it would make life easier.'

So Judy picked up the script and Vlad flew up and sat by Judy, mopping his brow.

'Gosh, that was hard work!' he said, and then whispered, 'Poor old Vlad, Poor little Drac.'

'Why are you whispering?' asked Judy.

'So the Lord High Executioner won't hear me,' answered the vampire.

Judy giggled, 'Do you mean Dad?'

'Who else?' said Vlad. 'It's my private name for him.'

'Well, don't let him hear you,' said Judy. 'He'll get angry.'

'It'll be our secret,' said Vlad. 'Just between you and me. Now, let's read through this script and see what sort of star part I've got.'

So Judy started to thumb through the script.

'I don't see much in it about vampires,' she told Vlad. 'There seem to be lots of other monsters though. Look, there's Frankenstein and a dinosaur and several robots, a magnetic octopus, an electronic stingray, four space sharks, a dragon that spurts flames at both ends and a fleet of Deadly-Ray Saturn-dominated Mastodons.'

'What are they?' asked Vlad, looking very confused.

'I don't know,' confessed Judy. 'I think we'd best talk to Malcolm Meilberg about this.'

'Well, yes,' said Vlad. 'I mean, I'm the star. I can't understand it at all. This script should be all about vampires.'

'It's very odd,' agreed Judy. 'Still, as it's your first day on the set tomorrow, your very first day of filming, you can ask Malcolm Meilberg yourself.'

'I will,' said Vlad. 'I most certainly will. You can bet your bottom dollar on that.'

'I can't get over you actually making a film,' Judy went on excitedly. 'It's what you always wanted to do. Do you remember when we first found you under the stone? That's why you wanted to come to London, to be a famous film star.'

'That's right,' agreed the vampire. 'What a long time ago it seems. I bet your never thought I'd make it.'

'I never did,' said Judy.

'I've done well, haven't I?'

'You certainly have, Vlad,' said Judy.

'Still,' confessed Vlad, 'I'm a bit scared about tomorrow. I wish you could come with me.'

'So do I, but Mum and Dad would never let me have a day off school.'

At that moment Paul came in. 'What's all this about a day off school?'

'Nothing,' said Judy. 'It's just that it's Vlad's first day of filming tomorrow and he'd like us to be there to hold his hand, but I don't think Mum and Dad would let us have the day off.'

'Worse luck,' groaned Paul. 'I'd give anything to see a film being made, particularly by Malcolm Meilberg!'

'No chance of Mum and the Lord High Executioner allowing you to stay away?' asked Vlad.

'None,' said Judy.

'Absolutely none,' agreed her brother.

'Hmmm,' said Vlad. 'I've got an idea. Just hand me the phone, Judy dear, I've got a couple of phone calls to make.'

So Vlad dialled a number while Judy and Paul gazed at him, wondering what he was up to.

'Hiya, Mal,' said Vlad. 'Vlad here. Oh, I'm fine. *Me* worried about tomorrow? You must be joking! No, not a bit, you forget I've been performing for tourists for years. Your little film's a piece of cake as far as I'm concerned.

'Why I was phoning was that I think a bit of publicity might come in useful. You agree? Oh, good! Well, what I was thinking was that if Judy and Paul and some of their school friends could be on the set tomorrow, it might catch the public eye. You know the sort of thing, "Modern Monsters Meet Merry Mates" or "Meilberg Makes Clever Classes Keen". Yes, that sort of thing. Yeah – good – great – alright – I'll tell them they can come. Thanks a million, Mal. See you on the set tomorrow. Bye!

'He says you can come!'

'Well done, Vlad!' said Paul, getting very excited.

'You haven't heard anything yet,' said Vlad as he dialled another number.

'Hello. Vlad the Drac speaking. Can I have a word with the head teacher, please?'

'*Our* head teacher?' asked Judy.

Vlad nodded. 'Oh, good afternoon, Mrs Thompson,' said the vampire in his most polite tone. 'So sorry to bother you, I know how busy you are, but the most wonderful educational opportunity has cropped up for your children. Yes, I knew you'd be interested. Malcolm Meilberg would like to show two classes of children how a film is made. Well quite, it would be most educational. Have a good time as well? Heaven forbid, no this would be an entirely educational experience. Good, excellent! So Paul and Judy's classes can come to the film studios tomorrow? That's wonderful. I'll see to it that they all learn a lot. Thank you so much. Byeee.'

'Gosh,' said Judy, 'that was neatly done.'

'Think nothing of it, dear girl,' said Vlad. 'Just leave everything to your Uncle Vlad!'

The next day a car came to take Vlad off to the film studio. When he arrived on the set he was taken straight to Malcolm Meilberg.

'Hi there, Vlad. Welcome to the set,' said Malcolm Meilberg, taking off his sunglasses. 'Come on in and let's have a chat about the script.'

'Yes, I want to talk about that,' said Vlad. 'I couldn't see much of a part in it for a vampire.'

'Not much of a part?' exclaimed Malcolm Meilberg. 'It's a *great* part, Vlad. The vampire says, "I nicked him down at Puddle Rock".'

'Is that all?' asked Vlad, his face falling.

'Is that all? *Is that all?!* Listen, Vlad, it's a great part, really great! It's not how much you say in the movie business, it's what you say and how you say it. That is the most important line in the whole film.'

'Still,' said Vlad sulkily, 'it's not much of a part.'

'Come on,' said the film producer. 'Just imagine there are two space ships: one is full of monsters representing the powers of good and helping the Princess Melita; the other is a terrible black space ship full of evil monsters working for the powers of evil and darkness, represented by the Dagathon the Kolgat.'

'Oh,' said Vlad. 'And is the vampire a good monster or a bad monster?'

'He's good, real good. Frankenstein and the

vampire and a dinosaur and several robots are helping the princess.'

'Oh,' said Vlad, a bit disappointed. 'So I'm a goodie?'

'You sure are,' said Malcolm Meilberg. 'And the baddies in the other spaceship are King Kong, a Mastodon, three flying sharks and two thousand sting-ray ants. But you, Vlad, you will be the only real monster. All the others will be fakes.'

'It's still a very small part,' complained Vlad. 'I want to be the star. Poor old Vlad, Poor little Drac.'

'You're not allowed to say that,' reminded Malcolm Meilberg.

'I am when the Lord High Executioner isn't around.'

'Who?' asked Malcolm Meilberg, puzzled.

'Dad,' explained Vlad. 'It's my special name for him.'

'I see,' said Malcolm Meilberg. 'Well, I suppose I should begin by introducing you to some of the people you'll be working with.'

So Vlad went around the set on Malcolm Meilberg's shoulder, complaining loudly that there weren't any vampires working on the set.

'This is our script writer, Graham Brown,' said Malcolm Meilberg.

Vlad looked hard at Graham Brown.

'Have you ever thought of changing your name?' he asked the writer.

'Well, er . . . no,' said Graham Brown, looking surprised.

'Well you should,' said Vlad. 'You should be called Snodgrass. I myself was nameless for some time and then called myself Vlad the Drac because it suited me. Now there is no way your unfortunate parents could have known that you would turn into a Snodgrass who didn't write proper parts for vampires, but a Snodgrass you have become and you might as well accept the fact.'

'See you later, Graham,' said Malcolm Meilberg hurriedly. 'Come on, Vlad. Come and meet our designer, Fred Jones.'

'Doesn't like designing vampires much, does he?' commented Vlad. 'And he's no Fred Jones, his name should be Podsnap.'

''Scuse us, Fred,' said Malcolm Meilberg hastily. 'We're in a hurry right now.'

In his rush to get Vlad away, Malcolm Meilberg bumped into a girl.

'Hi there, Sally. This is Vlad the Drac. Meet Sally Smith, our make-up girl.'

'She's not making *me* up,' said Vlad. 'I'm a real vampire. I don't need make-up like those other monsters, and she shouldn't be called Smith, Slugberry's the name for her.'

'You'd better not call me that,' said Sally Smith and she walked away.

'Have it your own way, Slugberry!' Vlad called after her.

'You've got to stop this, Vlad,' said the film producer as they came to a door marked 'A. Snowman.'

'A. Snowman!' yelled Vlad hooting with laughter, 'The Abominable, I presume!'

At that moment a man opened the door.

'This is Mr Anthony Snowman, our cameraman,' said Malcolm Meilberg nervously.

'Yes, that's right, and if you're going to call me silly names you needn't expect me to bother to see that you film well!' said Mr Snowman as he slammed the door.

By the time Judy and Paul and the other children showed up on the set everyone was fed up and angry because Vlad had been so rude. Malcolm Meilberg explained the situation to the children.

'He called the writer "Snodgrass", the designer "Podsnap", the make-up girl "Slugberry" and the cameraman "The Abominable". I don't know how we're going to get this film made if he goes on like this.'

'Give him a taste of his own medicine,' suggested Judy.

'You mean give him a name *he* won't like?' asked Malcolm Meilberg, brightening up. 'Good thinking.'

'I've got it,' said Paul. 'Let's call Vlad "Boris the Bat".'

Judy giggled. 'He won't like it one bit.'

'That,' said Malcolm Meilberg, 'that is the idea.'

'Well,' said Mrs Thompson, the teacher. 'I think Vlad is behaving very badly and needs to be taught a lesson. Let's make up a song about Boris the Bat.'

So by the time Vlad flew over to meet Paul and Judy and the children, they had all learned the song and were singing:

'Here comes Boris,
Boris the Bat,
Dear old Boris,
Doing this and that.

Here comes Boris,
Boris the Ghoul,
Dear old Boris,
Playing the fool.

Here comes Boris,
Doing his thing,
Dear old Boris,
Having a fling.

Here comes Boris,
Boris the Bat,
Dear old Boris . . .'

At this point Vlad interrupted. 'Who is this Boris everyone is talking about? Who is he? Some silly monster with a bigger part than me? You must be bonkers, singing silly songs about some silly bat called Boris.'

At that moment a boy came in shouting, 'Boris, Boris the Bat, calling Boris the Bat, you're wanted on set immediately!'

'He must be barmy,' declared Vlad. 'He seems to think that *I'm* Boris the Bat. Who is this Boris?'

'You,' chorused all the children.

'Me,' exclaimed Vlad in horror. 'But my name's Vlad the Drac. I chose it myself.'

'But we all think that Boris suits you better,' explained Mrs Thompson. 'We discussed it with Snodgrass and Podsnap and Slugberry and The Abominable, and they all agree that Boris is much more suitable than Vlad.'

Vlad burst into tears. 'But I don't like Boris, I want to be called Vlad,' he wailed and he buried himself in Judy's hair.

'Well Boris, look at it like this. There won't be a problem if you call everyone by their proper names. Then everyone will call you Vlad.'

'It's not fair,' complained Vlad. 'I gave all those people really interesting names, not silly ones like Boris. The same old story, people win out again. I suppose I'll have to agree. Poor old Boris, Poor little Vampire.'

'Well done, Judy,' said Malcolm Meilberg. 'You certainly solved our problem.'

'So Boris was your idea,' moaned Vlad. 'So you

are a person after all. I should have known. Great Uncle Ghitza was right when he said to me, "Vlad my boy, never trust anyone, not anyone, least of all a human being." I should have listened. He was a wise old vampire, my Great Uncle Ghitza. In fact, if people had any sense they'd make a film about him and then there'd be a star part for me. But I'm disappointed in you, Judy, very disappointed. I shall have to put you high on my list for vampirising.'

4

Alas Poor Frankenstein

By the time they got home that night, Vlad had forgotten to be cross with Judy, but he was still cross about his part.

'I've hardly got a part at all,' he moaned to Judy. 'I thought I was going to be a superstar, but instead I'm just one monster among many, with one mangy line.'

'It sounds alright to me,' said Judy. 'You're getting paid a lot of money.'

'That's not the point at all,' complained the vampire. 'And it's *not* alright. I mean, the others aren't even real.'

'What do you mean, not real?' asked Judy.

'You may well ask, you may well ask. For a start there's Frankenstein, he's just like a big suit of armour. Then there are the robots, a dinosaur which is a silly rubber model, and they've even got a female monster! It's an – an Egyptian mummy!'

Judy giggled. 'Vlad, mummies aren't necessarily female.'

'Oh, no?' retorted Vlad. 'Then what are they?'

'Mummies were the way the ancient Egyptians preserved their dead. They took out the dead person's insides and put herbs in instead, and then they bandaged the body to preserve it.'

'Ugh!' said Vlad, pulling a face. 'It sounds awful. That just goes to show how long people have been horrible. Vampires don't do things like that.

'But what am I going to do, Judy? I can't be upstaged by robots and bandages. How could I ever face the children? I told Mrs Vlad and the five little vampires that I was going to be a star. I can't disappoint them. You'll have to go and talk to Malcolm Meilberg and tell him that I should have a bigger part in the film. In fact, I think I should have the *biggest* part!'

'I don't think he'd listen to me, Vlad.'

'What am I going to do, Judy? What *am* I going to do? Poor old Vlad, Poor little Drac, Poor old Boris, Poor little Vampire.'

'Stop it!' snapped Judy. 'If Dad hears you, he'll go through the roof.'

At that moment Dad stuck his head round the door. 'If I hear what?'

'That I've got the smallest part in the film,' said Vlad quickly.

'That seems fair enough,' said Dad. 'You've got no acting experience. Judy, I've come to put up those shelves you asked for. Is this a convenient time for you?'

'Yes Dad, great!' said Judy. 'I'd like three, just about here.'

'Right,' said Dad. 'I'll just go and get my toolbox and we can get going.'

A few moments later Dad was back and measuring the wall for his shelves.

'Nobody bothers to ask if it's convenient for *me*,' complained Vlad. 'I'm having a major crisis in my career but do you care, no, you just carry on as though nothing as happened, Poor old . . .'

'Don't say it,' warned Dad.

'What I was going to say was, Poor old Boris, Poor little Vampire.'

Dad groaned and began to drill holes in the wall. Vlad began to complain about the noise but suddenly stopped and stared, fascinated, as Dad drilled.

'What are those for?' yelled Vlad above the noise.

'I'm making holes in the wall, so there are holes to put the screws into.'

'I see,' said Vlad thoughtfully. 'Think I'll stay and watch if you don't mind.'

'I don't mind,' said Dad.

So Vlad went and investigated the contents of Dad's tool-box, asking what each instrument was for, and then he declared that it looked more like a vampire's kit than a person's tool-box. Vlad tried some of the paint cleaner that was in the box but decided that he didn't like it, and then he watched Dad cut the wood for the shelves with his electric saw. Then Dad put the shelves up and an hour later the three of them stood back to admire Dad's handiwork.

'They're lovely, Dad,' grinned Judy. 'Thanks ever so much.'

'They look very good,' said Vlad, and he went back to investigating Dad's tool-box.

'Glad you all like them,' said Dad as he snapped the tool-box shut. 'Any time you want something doing, just let me know. I'm going downstairs to cook dinner now, see you later.'

When Mum came home they all sat down to supper. A place was laid for Vlad with a tube of hair conditioner as a special treat, to cheer him up. But Vlad was nowhere to be seen.

'If he can't be bothered to turn up when everyone else does,' said Dad, 'he can go without.'

The evening went on and still no Vlad. When it was time for Judy and Paul to go to bed, Judy told Mum she was worried.

'It's not like Vlad, Mum, to miss supper and not to be around *all* evening.'

'Maybe he's shut himself away to learn his lines,' suggested Mum.

'His line,' corrected Judy. 'He's very fed up because he's only got one line.'

'He would be!' said Mum. 'When did you last see him?'

Judy thought for a minute. 'It was when Dad put up those shelves in my room. Vlad was looking at Dad's tools, then Dad snapped the lid shut . . .'

Mum and Judy looked at each other in horror.

'Oh dear!' said Mum. 'Oh dear. Come on,' and together they went into the front room to find Dad.

'Dad, where's the tool-box? We think you shut Vlad in.'

'Oh no!' said Dad. Leaping up he cried, 'Quick, come on down to the cellar.'

All the Stones raced downstairs as quickly as possible and Dad pulled the box down from a shelf and opened it as fast as he could. There, fast asleep on top of a box of nails, lay Vlad.

'Vlad, I'm so sorry!' exclaimed Dad. 'We had no idea. Poor you, all alone in this dark, damp cellar.'

Vlad opened one eye and yawned. 'Don't mention it, old chap, I didn't mind one bit,' he said as he turned over and went to sleep again.

'That's odd,' said Dad. 'The one time he could have gone on about Poor old Vlad and all that and I *couldn't* have objected, and he missed his chance.'

'I think we'd better take him upstairs where it's warmer,' whispered Mum.

So very carefully they carried the vampire upstairs and put him in his drawer in Judy's room. The next morning Vlad woke up coughing and spluttering.

'Oh, poor Vlad,' said Judy. 'You must have caught cold in the cellar.'

'I feel very ill,' said Vlad. 'I can't possibly go and film today. 'You'll have to ring Mal up and tell him to save my line for another day.'

When Dad heard Vlad was ill he felt very guilty and said of course Vlad could stay at home and that as he was ill, presumably he'd sleep all day and not get into any trouble. Mum left Vlad a carton of his favourite scouring powder and all the Stones went off to school and to work.

Dad hurried home that afternoon in case Vlad felt worse, and when he opened the front door he could not believe his eyes. Every door in the house was off its hinges and lying on the floor. Dad rushed upstairs just in time to see Vlad drop a screwdriver and jump back into his drawer.

'Whatever are you doing?' yelled Dad. 'Unscrewing all my doors – what are you thinking of?'

'I don't know,' answered the vampire. 'I must have been sleep walking.'

'Come off it,' said Dad. 'I want a proper explanation.'

'I was feverish,' said Vlad. 'It's because you left me in that damp cellar.'

'I just don't understand why you did it,' said Dad.

'Well, I just wanted to practise unscrewing things.'

'Why?' asked Dad, puzzled.

'I just wanted to know if I could do it,' said the vampire. 'You never know when unscrewing something will come in handy.'

'Well, it was a loony thing to do!' shouted Dad. 'Just look at all those doors. You'd better get a little practice at screwing things back up again, and be quick about it before Mum comes home!'

'You'll have to help me,' said Vlad. 'I'm too small to hold the doors in position.'

'Oh, alright,' groaned Dad. 'Let's get on with

it. I'll hold this door, and you put the screws back in.'

By the time Mum and the children came home, everything was back in place. Over supper Dad told the family about Vlad's exploits.

'I still don't understand why you did it,' Dad told the vampire, 'but tomorrow you go to work on the film. No more days at home on your own for you.'

'Not necessary, old chap,' said the vampire.

'I thought you were supposed to be ill?' said Mum.

'I've had a miraculous recovery,' Vlad told her.

So the next day Vlad went to the film studios and came home absolutely exhausted, refused supper and went straight to bed.

Later that evening there was a phone call from Malcolm Meilberg. Dad answered. After he put the phone down Dad told the family, 'Poor old Mal is very upset. Someone unscrewed Frankenstein, and they're going to have to work all night screwing him back together again. Who can have done such a thing? Who would have the motive to . . . V-l-a-d!'

Dad ran upstairs two at a time and burst into Judy's room. Vlad was sleeping deeply. Dad picked him up roughly.

'Do you know what happened to Frankenstein?' demanded Dad.

'No,' said Vlad innocently, rubbing his eyes. 'What happened?'

'He's been unscrewed!'

Vlad put his head in his hands. 'Alas poor Frankenstein, I knew him well.'

'You had nothing to do with it?'

'Me? No,' said Vlad in an amazed tone and shaking his head.

'I can't prove anything,' said Dad, 'but I have my suspicions.'

The next day Vlad went off filming again, and again he came home exhausted and went straight to bed.

That evening Malcolm Meilberg phoned again, very upset because someone had cut the points off the dinosaur's back with an electric saw. A team of people would be working all night to stick them back on, and hopefully the damage wouldn't show.

When Vlad was told he burst into tears.

'How do you think it makes me feel?' demanded the vampire. 'Knowing that some lunatic is attacking the monsters in "Marauding Monsters of the Outer Galaxy" – whoever it is may be after *me* next. Maybe I should be glad that I've only got a little part!'

After the accident to the dinosaur there were no more incidents and everyone began to settle down and forget about what had happened. Then it was Paul's birthday and he was given a computer. Vlad was fascinated by the computer and got Paul to teach him all about it.

'You show me everything you know,' said Vlad, 'and then you'll always have someone to play games with.'

Paul was delighted, so he and Vlad went right through the book of instructions together.

The day after Paul's birthday Malcolm Meilberg came round with a late birthday present. He seemed very depressed. Dad gave him a drink and asked him what was wrong.

'It's the monsters,' explained the film producer. 'One darn thing after another goes wrong. Honestly Nick, I don't see how I'm going to get this movie made. Someone is trying to sabotage the monsters.'

'I know,' said Mum sympathetically. 'Vlad is afraid whoever it is will be after him next.'

'Well, to be quite honest, I think that's a load of old flannel. He's suspect number one. But I don't see how he can have been responsible for this latest outrage.'

'What's happened now?' asked Dad.

'It's the robots. They've all been reprogrammed and are walking backwards on their heads. We've got three computer experts working on them now, but we're not sure if they'll be able to put them right. I've had to cancel tomorrow's filming. Still, this lets Vlad off the hook. He doesn't know anything about computers.'

'Oh yes he does,' said Paul. 'I showed him.'

'Is this a plot or something?' asked Dad.

'No Dad, honest. Vlad said he wanted to play computer games with me, so I went through the book with him.'

'Well, that puts the lid on it. Vlad is the saboteur,' said the film producer. 'What I don't understand is why he should want to do in all the monsters in his spaceship.'

'I think,' said Judy, 'that he hopes that if they're out of the way, you'll give him a bigger part.'

'Ah, I get you,' said Malcolm Meilberg. 'Well, no way. Either he stops being a wrecker or he is out on his ear.'

'I think you should tell him all this yourself,' said Dad.

So Vlad was brought downstairs and confronted with his crimes.

'Oh alright, I confess,' said Vlad. 'But I *had* to do it. I must have a bigger part. I told Mrs Vlad and the five children that I was going to be a star, and all I've got is one mangy line.'

'But Vlad,' explained Malcolm Meilberg, 'it's a very important part, and just having a real live vampire in the film will bring the crowds in. There will be cinema queues all over the world full of people waiting for a glimpse of the world's most famous vampire.'

'That's all well and good,' complained Vlad, 'but my public will want to hear me speak.'

'Look Vlad, it's not like that in this movie. Most of the dialogue is said by the humans; the Princess Melita, Ben Battler and Sorab Rusty-sword. The other monsters only grunt and rattle and screech, not a line between them.'

'I see,' sniffed Vlad. 'Everything for the people as usual. Now I understand.'

'I hope you do, Vlad,' said Malcolm Meilberg sternly. 'Because if you do anything else to the monsters, I'll write you out of the film. I'm going to take money out of your salary to pay for the damage you've already done. So you just watch your step – you just watch it.'

When Malcolm Meilberg had gone Vlad moaned to Mum, 'That Grottberger wasn't at all nice, taking money out of my salary indeed.'

'What's all this about Grottberger?' asked Mum, puzzled.

'It's my name for that Meilberg fellow.'

'Now Vlad, you've been told about names. You know it upsets people.'

'Oh I won't call him Grottberger to his face, only behind his back. It makes me feel better. Like you call the neighbours "Young Frankenstein" and "The Fruit Bowl on Legs".'

'Don't remind me,' said Mum.

Then Vlad began to walk around the kitchen table with a pronounced limp.

'What's up?' asked Mum.

'My leg, my leg, it hurts!' cried Vlad.

'Let me see,' said Mum quickly. 'Here, bend your knee, move your foot about. There, all alright – doesn't seem to be much wrong.'

'But it hurts!' shrieked Vlad. 'It needs to be bandaged up. I know it does. You're a doctor, you should know that.'

Mum sighed. 'Well, if you want a bandage I suppose I can manage that.'

Mum looked in her sewing box and found a bit of white tape. 'I can use this,' she said.

So Vlad let Mum bandage his leg. When she'd

finished he held his leg up and looked at it admiringly.

'All bandaged up,' he said. 'Just like a mummy. Well done, and now let's see if I can undo it.' And Vlad began to unravel the bandage.

'But Vlad, you've got a bad leg,' protested Mum, and then suddenly she realized. 'The mummy, you want to unbandage the mummy!' and she grabbed the lid of the cheese dish and slammed it down over Vlad, making him a prisoner.

'I won't let you out,' she declared, 'unless you promise me faithfully not to go near the mummy.'

Eventually Vlad agreed and was let out.

'You're very naughty, Vlad, to even think of it, and if I hear of anything happening to the mummy I'll refuse to have you in the house. Is that clear?'

'Everyone's ganging up on me,' complained the Vampire. 'How would you like to be edged out by a lump of metal, a slab of rubber, some silly robots and a big bandage?'

'What I would feel is not the point,' said Mum. 'Either you promise to behave or we'll send you back home.'

'Oh alright,' said the vampire grudgingly. 'And now I am going upstairs to my drawer to feel sorry for myself and I do not wish to be interrupted under *any* circumstances. I shall think whatever I like – even people can't object to thoughts.'

5

Vlad's Party

After a while Vlad got used to having only a small part and he began to enjoy filming.

One evening, the car that took Vlad to and from the studios drew up outside the house and Vlad and Malcolm Meilberg got out.

'Malcolm's bringing Vlad home,' Judy called and went to meet them at the door. Vlad came in on the film producer's shoulder and gave Judy a bunch of flowers. Malcolm Meilberg had an even bigger bunch for Mum.

'Would you like to stay to supper?' asked Mum. 'Pot luck.'

'Love to,' answered Malcolm Meilberg. 'I love home cooking and in my line of business, you don't get much of that.'

Soon they were all sitting round the kitchen table tucking into stew, except for Vlad who was sampling a new kind of hair shampoo.

'It's delicious,' exclaimed Malcolm Meilberg. 'You're a wonderful cook, as well as being pretty and clever and a wonderful mother. A toast to Mum everyone!'

So they all drank a toast to Mum. Mum glowed and looked very happy. Then Vlad cleared his throat and said:

'Silence, ladies and gentlemen, pray silence for his honour the Vlad.'

Everyone turned their attention to the vampire.

'We have just drunk a toast to Mum and quite right too, but now I would like to propose a toast to another member of this household, one who suffers – if not silently – suffers a great deal, who is sometimes quick to lose his temper but is always fast to forgive, a sensitive and creative creature but still lovable, ladies and gentlemen, I ask you to stand and join me in a toast to Vlad – I mean to DAD!'

So they all drank a toast to Dad, who was a bit confused, and giggled.

'Come on everyone,' yelled Vlad. 'Drink Romanian style. Don't put your glass down till you've finished it all. That's it.'

'What about us?' said Paul. 'What about a toast to us?'

'Quite right,' said Malcolm Meilberg. 'Ladies and gentlemen, lift your glasses in a toast to the two best children in this house – I give you Judy and Paul!'

So another glass of wine was drunk. Then Dad proposed a toast to Malcolm Meilberg and the success of 'Marauding Monsters of the Outer Galaxy'.

Then Vlad's feelings were hurt because no one had drunk a toast to him, so a toast was drunk to Vlad and Mrs Vlad and the five children and Great Uncle Ghitza. By that time they had got through three bottles of wine, and Dad got up to make some coffee.

'By the way,' said Vlad. 'It's my birthday next week and I would like to give a party.'

'It was your official birthday a few weeks ago,' protested Mum. 'And you said then that you didn't know when your real birthday was.'

'I don't,' said Vlad. 'This one is my unofficial birthday. I just pick any old date.'

'Where do you want to give this party?' asked Dad.

'Here, of course,' replied Vlad indignantly. 'This is where I live.'

'Oh no,' said Dad. 'Definitely not. Parties are very expensive.'

'I'd pay,' said Malcolm Meilberg.

'And it takes a long time to prepare for them,' Dad went on.

'We'd do it,' said Judy and Paul.

'And then there's all the clearing up,' said Dad, beginning to feel a bit desperate.

'I,' announced Vlad, 'will do the clearing up, every single bit, on my own.'

'We haven't given a party for years,' said Mum. 'I'd like to have one here. Who do you want to invite, Vlad?'

'Well,' said the vampire thoughtfully. 'Everyone who is working on the film, Snodgrass and Podsnap, Slugberry and the Abominable, and Grottberger of course.'

'Who's he?' asked Malcolm Meilberg.

'No one you would want to know,' replied Vlad

quickly. 'And we would invite all the stars, the Princess Melita and Ben Battler, and Sorab Rustysword, and your teacher Mrs Thompson, and my old friends the Punch and Judy man, PC Wiggins, the Hippy and that naughty pair who Vladnapped me last year, and I think we should have a children's party upstairs for my younger friends.'

'Good idea,' said Judy and Paul enthusiastically.

'I can see I've been overruled again,' groaned Dad.

'You certainly have,' said Malcolm Meilberg cheerfully.

'I can see why you were so lavish with the wine,' commented Dad.

'Vlad's idea,' Malcolm Meilberg told him.

'I should have known,' moaned Dad.

The invitations to the party were sent out and then Vlad decided that the house had to look as much like Dracula's castle as possible.

'Lots and lots of cobwebs,' he told Mum.

'But there aren't any cobwebs,' Mum pointed out.'

'I'll borrow some from the film studio,' said Vlad. 'And lots of coffins and ghosts and scaly monsters and big fat spiders and . . .'

'Not in my house,' said Mum firmly.

So Vlad had to settle for a few cobwebs and some rubber spiders. Mum looked at her nice house draped in cobwebs and pulled a face.

'It looks horrid,' she said.

''Course it does,' said Vlad. 'It's a monster party – the people will love it, you'll see.'

Vlad decided that he and Dad would put on a cabaret to entertain the guests.

On the day of the party the food arrived from a very expensive shop. Dad put the food out on the long table in the dining room. Judy and Paul looked at it in amazement.

'It must have cost a fortune – it looks delicious,' said Judy.

'Mmmm,' added Paul, 'finger lickin' good.'

Then the children helped Dad put out plates of cold meat and pies and salads and cakes and desserts.

'I'm going to put the wine punch in the middle,' said Dad, 'and the food can go all round.'

At that moment Vlad appeared carrying a batch of labels.

'I'm going to put them on the food,' he explained, 'so that all the people will know what they're eating,' and he flew over to some small chocolate cakes and put on a label saying 'Corpse cupcakes'. Then he flew on to a bowl of trifle and labelled it 'blood pudding', after that it was 'coffin cake', 'funeral fish fingers', 'hearse hamburgers', 'Mousse à la Mummy', 'Goulash à la Ghitza', 'Veal à la Vlad', 'Grandma Natalia's Curry', and on the punch he wrote 'Punch of Blood and Gore'.

'Ugh!' said Judy. 'I wouldn't want to eat *any* of that.'

'Who would?' said Dad.

'I wouldn't worry,' said Vlad cheerfully. 'If they don't like it, you can eat it all week and not have to buy any food, but they'll love it, you'll see.'

The guests began to arrive and they didn't seem to be put off by the 'Blood and Gore Punch'. When Vlad had greeted everyone, he went upstairs to make sure the children were having a good time. The children were playing 'Hide and Seek' when Vlad entered.

'Alright then,' Vlad announced, 'I shall hide now and after you have counted to ten, you come and look for me.'

The children dutifully counted ten and then went searching for Vlad. They invaded the grown-up party downstairs, but still no Vlad.

'I expect he forgot all about it,' said Mum. 'Start playing something else, and he'll turn up.'

So they started to play 'Musical Bumps', when suddenly a shriek came from the bathroom. Melinda Mason, who was playing the Princess Melita in the film, came rushing out.

'I was just checking my make-up,' she said, 'when I heard this shouting and banging.'

'You leave this to me,' said Dad and he went in to investigate.

'Let me out,' came muffled shouts.

'It's Vlad!' said Dad. 'But where is he?'

Paul giggled, 'I think he's in the cistern, Dad.'

So Dad opened the lid of the cistern and there sat Vlad looking very wet and fed up.

'You were supposed to come and look for me,' Vlad told Paul accusingly.

Hearse Hamburgers
PUNCH OF
BLOOD AND GORE
COFFIN CAKE

'We did,' Paul assured him, trying not to laugh, 'but we couldn't find you.'

'Well then,' said the vampire cheering up, 'I won.'

'You certainly did,' said Dad. 'Come on, we'll put you through the spin dryer.'

Vlad was soon dry and he went back upstairs to join in the 'Musical Bumps.' When the music stopped the children sat down as fast as they could. Judy heard shouts of 'Get up, you clumsy oaf, you're crushing me.'

Judy got up quickly and there was Vlad looking very disgruntled. 'Sorry Vlad, I just had to sit down very fast. It's how you play "Musical Bumps".'

'More like "Musical Squash the Vampire" if you ask me,' sulked Vlad.

So it was decided to play 'Pass the Parcel', and all the children sat in a circle and Vlad felt quite safe. They passed the parcel very carefully and when the music stopped, whoever had the parcel stripped off a layer of paper. In the end Judy's friend Lucy took off the last layer and won the prize.

'Let's play again,' yelled Vlad. 'She cheated, you all cheated.'

Mum came upstairs and called, 'Vlad, your guests are asking for you. You'd better come down.'

'Shan't,' said Vlad. 'I don't like people, they cheat.'

The children told Mum what had happened.

'I've got another parcel,' said Mum quickly. 'Play again, and I'll turn the music off this time.' So every time the parcel got to Vlad Mum stopped the record, and soon Vlad had won and was sitting on Mum's shoulder to go downstairs.

'I told you I'd win once there wasn't any cheating,' he told Mum.

'Yes, Vlad,' said Mum tactfully.

When Vlad got downstairs he began his cabaret. He got everyone to sing: 'Blood, blood, glorious blood', and then 'Humans and People, alive alive, O'. Then, although it was the wrong time of year, they sang Vlad's version of 'The Twelve Days of Christmas' ending up with:

'Great Uncle Ghitza brought to me,
A vampire up a gum tree.'

Then Vlad wanted to recite the 'Ode to Great Uncle Ghitza', but Dad thought it was too long for a party. So Vlad yelled 'Alright everyone, I am now going to teach you a vampire dance, "The Transylvania Trot".'

Vlad flew up on to the table and grabbed a spoon.

'You dance it like this,' he said, holding the spoon as if it was a partner. 'You take your partner and you go – slow, slow, quick, quick, bite – and then back – slow, slow, quick, quick, bite – and the lady bites the gentleman. Alright, everyone in twos now. Come on Snodgrass, you dance with Slugberry. Dad, you play the piano; Mum, you dance with Grottberger. Come on children, time for you to learn the dance of the vampire. Everyone ready? Good – now off you go. Slow, slow, quick, quick, bite, and a slow, slow, quick, quick, bite!'

Soon everyone was merrily dancing away. Vlad looked at them and laughed, then he threw away his spoon and began to dance on his own, kicking his legs up in the air and yelling,

'Everyone is doing it,
Doing it, doing it,
Everyone is doing it,
The Translyvania Trot.

I've got the people,
Doing it, doing it, doing it,
I've got all the people doing it,
The Transylvania Trot.

They look silly doing it,
Doing it, doing it,
They all look silly doing it,
The Transylvania Trot.'

At two in the morning the last guests left.

'Bye,' they called. 'Thanks for a really super, smashing, vampire party.'

'Just look at the mess,' sighed Mum, sitting down and taking her shoes off.

'You're not to even think about it,' instructed Vlad. 'I promised the party wouldn't cause you any work. You go to bed and have a nice lie-in tomorrow morning.'

When Mum and Dad came down at 11 o'clock

the next morning, the house was sparkling and clean, no sign of a party. Vlad was practising the Transylvania Trot on the kitchen table with a tin opener.

'Vlad, it looks wonderful!' cried Mum. 'How did you do it?

'Vampire magic,' grinned Vlad. 'Slow, slow, quick, quick, bite,' and he danced away clasping the tin opener.'

6

A Night at the Opera

One morning Vlad came downstairs to find six letters from Romania awaiting him. He looked at them.

'One from Mrs Vlad and one from each of the children. I'll open Mrs Vlad's first.'

'What has she got to say?' asked Mum.

'Not much,' said Vlad. 'Just that she and the children are missing me and all that. Now, let's see what the children have to say. "Dear Vlad the Dad" – that's what they call me – "We are all working hard and hope you enjoy being a star." Huh, they should only know the truth – "See you soon daddy," love and all that. Nothing interesting,' said Vlad. 'But they're good children. It's nice they remember their old dad.'

'There's another letter here,' said Judy, 'that you haven't opened yet. It's in a red envelope and it's got skulls drawn all over it.'

'That must be from young Ghitza,' exclaimed Vlad. 'He certainly is his Great Great Uncle's great great nephew. Let's see what he has to say. Ah yes, "Dear Vlad the Dad, I hope you are using every opportunity to vampirise as many people as possible. The others are working hard learning to read and other boring things, but I am working hard learning to be a very wicked vampire. I hope you'll have some juicy tips for me when you get home. Yours in Blood, Ghitza." He's such a naughty little vampire that one,' said Vlad proudly.

'It would be nice to meet your family some time,' said Mum. 'Properly though, not just for a moment like last time.'

'I'm not so sure you'd like to meet Ghitza,' said Vlad. 'You might not survive.'

'In the meantime,' Mum went on, ignoring him, 'I'd like to send your wife a note telling her that you're well and all that, and maybe a few small presents for the children. Though what I could get for Ghitza I cannot imagine.'

'Don't even try,' Vlad advised her.

'What's your wife's name?' asked Mum.

Vlad looked a bit puzzled. 'But you know her name. It's Mrs Vlad.'

'I don't mean that, I mean her own name – what you call her when you're on your own, like I'm Suzanne and you're Vlad.'

'Oh, she doesn't have a name like that,' Vlad assured Mum.

'She must have,' protested Mum. 'I mean, what was she called before she knew you?'

'No idea,' answered Vlad. 'I mean, her life didn't really begin until she met me, did it?'

'I don't believe it,' snapped Mum. 'When you got married I bet the magistrate didn't say, "Do you, Vlad, take this vampire, Mrs Vlad, to be your lawful wedded wife".'

'Jolly well did,' said Vlad.

'I don't believe you,' insisted Mum.

'Oh alright, don't believe me,' said the vampire, and he picked up the phone and asked to be put through to Romania. 'I'll ask her about her health and the children first,' said Vlad, 'and then I'll ask if she's got or has ever had a name of her own.'

When Vlad got through he chatted for a while in Romanian and then, covering the phone, he whispered, 'I'm going to ask her now.'

Mum and Judy listened intently, and suddenly they heard the sound of a woman's voice shouting down the phone. Then there was a bang as the phone was slammed down.

Vlad looked at the phone in amazement, then he turned to Mum. 'Her name is Magda and she was a bit cross.'

'I don't blame her,' said Mum. 'Imagine not knowing your own wife's name. Honestly Vlad, you are a nutter, you are really.'

'I know,' agreed Vlad. 'I'm an utter nutter.'

Just then the phone rang. Vlad picked it up.

'Hello, this is Vlad the Drac, the well known nutter. Oh hello, yes she is here, hang on – it's Dad,' said Vlad handing over the phone to Mum.

'Hello,' said Mum. 'Umm . . . Umm . . . oh, that sounds nice. I'll ask the children how they'd feel about it.' She turned to Paul and Judy and said, 'Dad's got some tickets for the ballet tonight, right in the front row. Do you want to go?'

'I'd love to,' said Judy.

'Oh, alright,' said Paul.

'Yes, they'd both like to go,' Mum told Dad. 'And so would I, so four seats would be wonderful.'

'That's right,' said Vlad. 'Don't ask me. Don't ask me if I wanted to go to the ballet.'

'What would a vampire do at the ballet anyway?' sneered Paul.

'Watch the dancing,' replied Vlad, 'just like all the rest of the audience.'

'Bet you don't know anything about ballet,' continued Paul.

'Jolly well do,' replied Vlad indignantly. 'As it happens, the ballet comes from Russia and that's right next door to Romania. And what's more, my Great Aunt Irena, Great Uncle Ghitza's wife, was a famous vampire ballet dancer, so there!'

'You can come if you want,' said Mum. 'We've got very good seats, right in the front row Dad said.'

'Thank you,' replied Vlad. 'I will be very happy to accompany you to the ballet.'

So that night the Stones and Vlad went to the ballet. They found their way to the four seats in the front row of the stalls, and the Stones sat down and began to look around for somewhere for Vlad to sit. Attached to the back of the seat between Judy and Dad was a metal ashtray.

'You could sit in that,' Dad suggested to Vlad.

'I don't want people stubbing their cigarettes out on me,' said Vlad.

'Don't worry about that,' said Dad. 'People

aren't allowed to smoke in here anymore. Those ashtrays are very old fashioned. They probably haven't been used for years.'

'Would you mind if our vampire sat in the ashtray?' Mum asked the people in the row behind.

'Why it's Vlad the Drac,' said the people in the next row. 'Gosh yes, *do* let him sit in the ashtray. Welcome to the ballet, Vlad.'

'Oh thank you, thank you,' said Vlad, glowing with delight and thrilled to be recognized.

So by the time the curtain went up, Vlad was seated comfortably on the ashtray with an excellent view of the stage. He sat and watched the dancers, his eyes wide with amazement.

'They're very good, aren't they?' he whispered to Judy.

'Yes, shush,' she whispered back.

In the interval they went into the bar. Everyone looked at Vlad sitting on Dad's shoulder and many people asked him to sign their programmes.

'I really do like the ballet,' Vlad informed the Stones, 'and I like the kind of people who come to watch the ballet too.'

After the interval the dancing started again. But about half way through the act, one of the ballerinas slipped and fell. Everyone in the audience coughed and looked at their programmes and pretended not to notice that anything had happened. Vlad looked at them in amazement. He stood up in his ashtray and looked at the rows of people behind, all studying their programmes intently.

'She fell over,' he announced in a loud voice. 'She fell over, and all the people here are pretending that nothing has happened. What a giggle!'

Then he turned back towards the stage. 'It's alright, love,' he called to the dancer, 'you just carry on – no one saw you fall – nothing happened – you just carry on dancing – nothing to worry about – you just keep going, dear!'

Dad grabbed Vlad, put him in his pocket and held on to him tight. Vlad struggled to get out but Dad didn't relax his grip. As soon as the ballet was over, Dad and the rest of the Stone family rushed for the exit. When they were out of the theatre Dad let Vlad out of his pocket.

'You didn't have to do that,' said the vampire indignantly. 'All I said was . . .'

'Don't repeat it,' said Dad. 'We all heard what you said only too well.'

'All I did was tell the truth, poor old Vlad . . .'

'Stop that!' snapped Dad. 'Come on, let's get out of here. Everyone is looking at us. You really disgraced us, Vlad – I've never been so embarrassed in all my life.'

Shortly after Vlad's exploits at the ballet, Malcolm Meilberg came to see the Stones and mentioned to Dad that he had a box at the opera. Would the Stones and Vlad like to come with him?

'You can't seriously imagine that I'd go to the opera with *him*,' said Dad, 'after the appalling way he behaved at the ballet. You can go with him if you want, but leave me out.'

'But Nick,' protested Malcolm Meilberg, 'I specially got the tickets because I knew it was one of your favourites.'

'I'd rather not go,' said Dad firmly. 'I'd rather never hear another opera again than go with Vlad. If he goes then I won't, it's me or him.'

'No problem,' said Vlad. 'I don't want to go to the opera, vampires don't like opera. Many times I heard Great Uncle Ghitza say that the only use for the opera was that it was a good place to vampirise people. No, you go without me, I shan't mind one bit. No problem, don't give it another thought.'

So it was arranged that the Stones would go to the opera with Malcolm Meilberg.

'It's not like Vlad to be so obliging and not complain,' said Mum.

'I think he's a bit ashamed about the way he behaved at the ballet and wants to make up for it,' said Judy.

'I don't believe it,' said Dad. '*I* think he's up to no good.'

But as the evening for the visit to the opera approached, Vlad was very helpful and obliging.

'You lot go off and have a good time. I'll just go and have a kip in my tool-box bed in the cellar. It's just like Dracula's coffin, I'll enjoy that.'

And as the Stones were leaving and they called goodbye to Vlad, there was no reply.

'I expect he's already asleep in the cellar,' said

Mum, and they all climbed into the car which Malcolm Meilberg had sent to take them to the opera. Dad couldn't stop worrying about what Vlad might be up to, but everyone tried to reassure him.

'Don't let it get to you, Nick,' said Malcolm Meilberg. 'Stay cool and just let yourself enjoy your night at the opera.'

When they got to the opera house they were taken to their box. The opera began, and Judy and Paul were soon a bit bored for they found it rather hard to follow the plot, but Mum and Dad and Malcolm Meilberg enjoyed it. Paul was getting restless, and he yawned and began to look around when suddenly he noticed a small head sticking out of Mum's handbag and watching the stage with interest and amusement. Paul kicked Judy gently and pointed to Vlad. Judy nodded and the two children sat nervously through the first act, hoping Vlad would behave. When the interval came Judy said:

'Mum, I think we've got an extra creature in this box,' and she pointed to Mum's bag. Vlad grinned.

'Evening all. You didn't really think you could go off and leave me behind while you were having a good time. I fooled you all.'

'As long as you're quiet, we don't mind too much,' said Malcolm Meilberg. 'If you want to sit quietly and enjoy the music, that's alright.'

'He was quiet until after the interval last time,' Mum pointed out.

Vlad sat quietly watching the opera until the last act when the hero lay dying in the arms of his wife, who was disguised as a boy. The hero began to sing his farewell, but this was too much for Vlad.

'He's singing,' said the vampire loudly. 'He's supposed to be dying, and he's singing. I mean, I know people are silly, that they do some pretty peculiar things but no one, absolutely no one, sings when they're dying. This is daft. And look at that woman. No one could ever take her for a boy. She's got the most enormous . . .'

Malcolm Meilberg grabbed Vlad, threw him into Mum's bag, snapped it shut and sat on it. As soon as the opera was over they raced out.

'How could you do such a thing?' yelled Dad. 'It's too much!'

'All I did was tell the truth. People can't take that. Poor old Vlad and all that.'

'And I can't take any more. Mal, as a friend

I'm begging you, please, please finish this film so that Vlad can go home. I've had enough. I can't take any more. If this sort of thing goes on I won't be able to answer for my actions!' cried Dad.

'We've nearly finished, Nick,' said Malcolm Meilberg soothingly. 'Don't worry, I'm sure Vlad won't get up to any more mischief.'

'Famous last words,' moaned Dad.

7

Top of the Pops

'Today's the day,' Vlad announced at breakfast soon afterwards.

'The day for what?' asked Dad.

'The day I say my line,' said Vlad.

'What is this famous line of yours, Vlad?' Dad asked.

'Oh it's eh . . . umm . . . let me see . . . oh dear. Yes, I did know it, I really did. Don't say a word, it's coming, it's coming. Yes, "I nicked him down at Puddle Rock".'

'That's an odd line,' commented Dad frowning.

'Well you see, the vampire comes back to the goodies' spaceship with a triple ray spiked craberdonian as prisoner and he says, "I nicked him down at Puddle Rock".'

'Oh, I see,' said Dad. 'Well, I hope you get it right.'

'Of course I'll get it right,' replied Vlad indignantly and he swept off into the waiting car.

As it was now the school holidays, Paul and Judy were allowed to go with Vlad to watch the filming. For Paul it was a dream come true, and he watched fascinated as the set of the inside of the spaceship was prepared for filming, and the lights were set up and the make-up put on the actors. When everything and everyone was ready, Malcolm Meilberg was ready to shoot the scene.

'Alright, everyone on the set,' he called. 'Filming take 45, sound, camera, action!'

As the cameras started to film the spaceship everyone was wondering what had happened to the vampire. Suddenly there was a banging on the door of the spaceship and one of the robots opened the door after Ben Battler had asked for the password and got the right reply. Slowly the door was lowered and in staggered Vlad carrying the triple ray spiked craberdonian.

'Where did you get that?' asked Ben Battler.

'I sicked him down by Suddle Sock,' Vlad replied.

'CUT!' yelled Malcolm Meilberg. 'OK, Vlad, take it again.'

So they started the whole scene again, but the next time Vlad said, 'I picked him up at Puddle Pock.'

'CUT!' yelled Malcolm Meilberg. 'Alright, Vlad. Now say the line to me slowly and quietly in your own time, "I nicked him down at Puddle Rock".'

'"I kicked him down at Ruddle Dock",' said Vlad. 'No, hang on, "I licked him down at Luddle Lock". No, "I flicked him down at Fluddle Mock".'

Malcolm Meilberg groaned. 'Maybe we'd better just film this sequence another day.'

'No,' pleaded Vlad, 'just give me one more

chance. Please, please, Mal. I'll get it right next time, I know I will.'

'Well, alright Vlad, just once more. Ready for the take, everyone. Here we go. Sound, camera, action!'

This time Vlad came in with the triple ray spiked craberdonian and announced:

'I micked him down at Muddle Mock.'

'CUT!' shrieked Malcolm Meilberg and buried his head in his hands. 'I can't stand it – this film is never going to be finished. OK everyone, have a day off. We'll re-schedule the filming and do this scene later on.'

On the way home Vlad was very miserable.

'I felt such a fool,' he told Paul and Judy. 'I mean, everyone was there. Old Grottberger was yelling and screaming, the Abominable was working the cameras, and Snodgrass and Podsnap and Slugberry were all there.'

'I expect you just got nervous, Vlad,' said Judy soothingly.

'Well, I did,' said the vampire, 'and once you've made a mistake, it gets worse each time. Oh dear, oh dear.'

After that, Vlad wasn't wanted on the set for a couple of days and he began to make secretive phone calls.

'What's he up too?' asked Dad suspiciously.

'Don't be so distrusting,' said Judy. 'Maybe it's something good.'

'Maybe,' said Dad, 'and maybe not.'

However, nothing good or bad happened until

one evening when Vlad came home in his official car and Paul let him in. Paul took one look at Vlad and roared with laughter.

'Vlad, you look horrible. Whatever have you done to yourself?'

'I have been to the hairdresser and had a green mohican,' replied Vlad glaring at Paul. 'I'd have thought that was perfectly obvious.'

'You look absolutely awful,' declared Paul. 'Whatever did you do that for?'

'I have just made a video for "Top of the Pops" said the vampire, 'and I wanted to look more with it, more hip, more trendy, more mod and all that jazz. I felt my image was a bit old-fashioned.'

'When is this video going to be on?' asked Paul. 'I can't wait to see it.'

'Well, you won't have to,' said the vampire. 'As it happens, it's going to be on in about half an hour. Malcolm Meilberg may not think much of my talents, but "Top of the Pops" were very impressed. This time I'm the star and no messing.'

'Oh good,' said Paul, still trying not to laugh. 'We'd better get ready to watch it then.'

'Better had,' agreed Vlad.

So half an hour later Judy, Paul, Mum and Vlad sat in front of the T.V.

'Where's the Lord High Executioner?' asked Vlad.

'Who?' said Mum.

'Your husband, Ma'am,' explained Vlad.

'What an odd thing to call him,' said Mum.

'Anyway, he's not coming home from rehearsals until later.'

'Trust him to be out during my moment of glory.'

The three of them watched 'Top of the Pops'. The programme was much as usual until the DJ said 'And now folks, something entirely new and different. Number 96 in the charts but climbing all the time "You're my vampire baby" by Vlad the Drac and the Sanguine Seven!'

Filling the screen was a huge castle. Eerie music began, voices in loud whispers called, 'Vlad, Vlad, where are you, Vlad?' The castle was covered with a huge cobweb and Vlad was trapped on the web, but gradually he bit his way through it, the web fell away and the music really began. Vlad flew round the castle and then landed on the roof where there was a set of drums and the members of a rock group all standing in coffins. Vlad picked up the drum sticks and began to play with great energy and delight. Often he abandoned his sticks and jumped up and down on the drums and kicked the cymbals.

'Good thing Dad wouldn't let you bring those things into the house,' said Mum above the noise.

'Quiet,' said Vlad. 'Listen to the music.'

The lead singer jumped up and down in his coffin, strummed his guitar and began to sing:

> 'Vampire, vampire,
> Come to me.
> You're my honey,
> Can't you see.

Vampire, vampire
Flying in the night.
Vampire, vampire,
Give me a fright.

Vampire, vampire,
Come close to me.
Vampire, vampire,
I love you, you see.

Vampire, vampire,
Give me a bite.
Vampire, vampire
Come into the light.'

Then all the musicians were joined in the chorus by a lot of girls dressed as vampires:

'Vampire you are the one,
Vampire you block out the sun,
Vampire you're the one for me,
Vampire, I love you, you see.
Yeah, yeah, yeah, yeah.'

After that the music continued, Vlad floated down in front of the castle and fell into a pram. The girl vampires began to push the pram round the castle, the coffins began to circle round the castle, then one by one they disappeared into the darkness. Then only Vlad and the girls were left, Vlad flew out of the pram and vampirised them all. As they lay on the ground Vlad sang:

'I was your vampire baby,
And I don't mean maybe,
I was your vampire baby,
But, I've vampirised you now.'

Then Vlad squirted tomato sauce over everyone and the screen was covered in ketchup and that was the end. The audience in the studio cheered and cheered. Vlad joined in at home.

'That was jolly good, wasn't it?' Vlad said to the Stones.

'You were very good,' they told him.

'It was a bit odd,' said Mum.

'Oh, Mum,' said Paul and Judy together. 'It wasn't odd at all. All modern videos are like that. It was great, Vlad.'

Vlad beamed and announced that all that vampirising had given him an appetite. Mum decided to serve supper and put Dad's in the oven for when he came back. Vlad tucked into his washing-up liquid and talked about being a pop star.

Dad came home tired and a bit grumpy about half way through supper.

'I don't know why you had to do that to your hair,' he told Vlad. 'You look revolting.'

'It's a very suitable look for a pop star,' said Vlad.

'It just looks awful to me,' said Dad. 'In fact, you're putting me off my supper.'

'Dad!' said Judy and Paul.

'Oh Nick, you're being very unkind,' protested Mum.

'Well, it's true!' said Dad. 'I can't enjoy my supper with that green thing sitting on the other side of the table.'

Vlad burst into tears. 'I shall go and sit in the tool-box,' he announced. 'I don't want to be where I'm not appreciated.' And he flounced out.

A little later Malcolm Meilberg came round.

'That vampire,' he said, 'is driving me crazy. I turn on the TV tonight and what do I see but Vlad with a green Mohican. How am I going to fit that into my movie – for half the film the vampire has black hair and then suddenly and for no reason at all he has a green mohican! The two bits of film won't fit together.'

'Couldn't you kill the vampire off in the film?' suggested Dad.

'Well, I could,' said the film producer, 'but Vlad wouldn't be too happy about that. Just a moment though. You just gave me an idea. Yeah, it's great – I just need to sell it to Vlad.'

So Vlad was persuaded to come up from the cellar, Dad apologised and made Vlad some hot toothpaste as a special treat, then Malcolm Meilberg told Vlad of his plan.

'Vlad, I want you take a very special part in the film.'

'Oh yes?' said Vlad. 'Tell me about it.'

'Well, it's like this. The vampire leaves the spaceship and goes to look for a triple ray spiked craberdonian at Puddle Rock. He knows it's dangerous, but he's so devoted to the princess he takes the risk, because he's very brave and he knows the power of good must triumph. So he leaves the others and goes alone into space.'

'Yes?' said Vlad.

'Then,' said Malcolm Meilberg, 'after days away, they've all given him up for dead. Everyone is grieving because the vampire was so good . . .'

'Yes?' said Vlad.

'Then one day they hear a faint tap on the door. They rush to open it, and the vampire staggers in . . .'

'Yes?' said Vlad.

'And he's got a green mohican and everyone on the spaceship knows what that means . . .'

'Yes?' said Vlad.

'It means that the triple ray spiked craberdonians were waiting in an ambush and they got him, and they've put him through a machine to make him betray the princess. The others on the spaceship don't know whether he talked or not.'

'Yes?' said Vlad.

'But the vampire is dumb, totally dumb. The green mohican treatment means you go dumb, so the vampire writes the Princess Melita a note assuring her that he has told the powers of darkness nothing. Then he dies in her arms.'

'The vampire dies to save the spaceship?' asked Vlad.

'That's it, and everyone weeps.'

Tears rolled down Vlad's face. 'They all cry because the vampire is so good and brave,' he sobbed.

'That's it!' said Malcolm Meilberg. 'And when

he's dead, all the creatures in the spaceship talk about him.'

'Everyone talks about him?' said Vlad.

'That's right,' said Malcolm Meilberg. 'All the time, even though he's gone in body, he's there in spirit right until the very end of the film.'

'Right until the end,' said Vlad. 'That sounds wonderful. A film about a brave and noble vampire, now that's what I call a plot. And I don't mind not having a speaking part, now that I'm a very famous pop star.'

8

Exit Vlad

'Good morning, Flunglebunge,' said Vlad. 'Come on, get up. I want someone to play with.'

Judy yawned and tried to wake up. 'Aren't you filming today, Vlad?' she asked sleepily.

'No, filming is all over. Yesterday they filmed the scene in which I died in the arms of the Princess Melita, so now I'm out of the film except that they talk about me all the time, about me being so brave and everything.'

'Oh,' mused Judy. 'So you'll be at home all the time then?'

'That's right, my little Flunglebunge.'

'What's all this "Flunglebunge"?' asked Judy.

'It's a new vampire word I made up.'

'Is a Flunglebunge nice or nasty?'

'Well,' said Vlad, 'when I call you "my little Flunglebunge" and nibble your ear it's nice, but if I say you stupid, knock-kneed, goggle-eyed Flunglebunge then it isn't nice. It's one of those useful words, it means different things at different times.'

'I see,' said Judy. 'I'm Flunglebunge and Dad's the Lord High Executioner.'

'I call him "The Lord High" for short,' said Vlad.

'Why only Dad and me?' asked Judy. 'Why doesn't Paul have a special name?'

'Oh he does,' Vlad assured her. 'It's either Bungleboots or Bunglebonce, I can't decide.'

'They're funny names,' said Judy.

'Well,' explained the vampire, 'I've never liked Paul as much as I like you, and then he went and told on me. He told Grottberger and the Lord High that I knew all about computers and got me into trouble. He's useless that boy, useless, from his bonce to his boots.'

'Oh, he's alright,' said Judy laughing. 'So what is it going to be, Bungleboots or Bunglebonce?'

'I think,' said Vlad, frowning hard, 'that I shall call Paul Bunglethorpe. What do you think of that then, Judy? I mean Flunglebunge.'

Judy laughed. 'It's rather good, Vlad. So there's the Lord High and his two children Flunglebunge and Bunglethorpe.'

'That's it,' said Vlad.

'And what about Mum. What are you going to call her?'

Vlad looked shocked. 'Oh, she's just Mum. No funny names for her.'

At breakfast Vlad chatted away, calling Judy 'Flunglebunge', and Paul 'Bunglethorpe'. Judy thought it was funny but Paul was furious.

'I don't like being called silly names. My name's Paul and that's the only name I'll answer to, Boris.'

As it was the summer holidays, Vlad spent

the day playing with the children. In the afternoon they went cycling and Vlad sat in Judy's basket and enjoyed the ride. On the way back, Vlad wanted to go on Paul's bike and Paul agreed if Vlad promised not to call him silly names. So Vlad transferred himself to the basket on Paul's bike and began to give loud instructions.

'Turn right, no not here – there! Slow down, careful, traffic lights ahead, you're going too fast, watch it, brake, brake – look where you're going – eyes on the road – watch that lorry, easy now!'

Paul drew up. 'You'll have to take him again, Judy,' said an exasperated Paul. 'I can't stand it, he's a back basket driver.'

So Judy took Vlad back, and he shouted at Paul from Judy's basket. 'Bunglebonce, stupid old Bungleboots, idiot Bunglethorpe, I don't want to go in your rotten old basket anyway!'

'Silly old Boris,' Paul retorted. 'Stupid old bat!'

'Stop it you two!' said Judy.

'Well I'm fed up,' said Paul. 'He thinks he can do and say whatever he likes. I wish he'd go home.'

The next day Paul and Vlad weren't talking. Mum had gone to work and Dad had gone out to do the weekly shop. Vlad announced that he was having a publicity session.

'You know the sort of thing,' he said to Judy. 'Photographs and interviews with Vlad the

Drac, the world famous superstar, Pop Singer and actor. It's a good thing my green mohican has grown out, though.'

'It did grow very quickly,' Judy commented.

'I know,' agreed Vlad. 'Vampire hair grows very, extra-super-specially fast.'

'Where are you going for your publicity session?' asked Judy.

'I'm not going anywhere,' said Vlad. 'They're coming here.'

'Have you asked Dad?' enquired Judy.

'The Lord High? No, why should I?'

'Well, it is his house,' said Judy. 'He'll be furious.'

'Don't worry, my little Flunglebunge, I'll deal with it, if and when it's necessary.'

Later that day huge vans drew up outside the house. Soon the Stone household was full of lights and cameras, make-up people, people operating the lights and the cameras, producers and the director and the interviewer. Vlad lay back on a cushion on the couch in the front room and chatted to his admirers.

'Yes, *do* go into the kitchen and make tea,' he told someone. 'Drinks over there, help yourselves, make yourselves at home. Yes, do smoke, that's fine, use that vase over there as an ashtray.'

Judy and Paul sat in the corner as Vlad was interviewed and filmed. He was holding forth on his life as a star and on relations between vampires and people when there was a crash and the bright television lights went out. Paul and Judy leapt up and there, sprawled on the hall floor, was Dad.

'Oh dear,' said Paul. 'Dad slipped on the wires as he came in with the shopping.'

Vlad got up indignantly and flew to the door. 'You've ruined my publicity session,' he declared. 'All the lights are out, you clumsy old nogbert. Honestly!' Then, turning to the lighting people he demanded, 'How long will it take you to get this lot set up again?'

'What's going on here?' asked Dad getting up off the floor.

'Vlad's having some publicity photographs and interviews done,' explained Paul nervously.

'Is he now?' said Dad, rubbing his elbow. 'We'll see about that. And what's happening in the kitchen?'

'The T.V. people are making snacks and tea and things,' Paul told him.

Dad went up to Vlad. 'Now what is going on?' he demanded. 'These people seem to have taken over my house. Who said they could have a go at my drinks?'

'I did,' said Vlad.

'And who said they could smoke?'

'I did,' said Vlad.

'And who said they could cook in my kitchen?'

'I did,' said Vlad.

'Well, I think you've got a nerve!' yelled Dad.

'You are interrupting my publicity session,'

declared Vlad. 'Now go upstairs and stay out of the way until all these people have gone, and don't go into the toilet because it's been turned into a dark room to develop pictures of me.'

'You mean I can't even use my own lavatory?' shouted Dad. 'You've gone too far, finally you have gone *too* far. Alright everyone, time to go. Pack up, come on, get all this stuff out of here, this is a private house. Come on – all out, cameras, lights, out all of you.'

'You're ruining my publicity session!' yelled Vlad.

'And you're ruining my home,' Dad shouted back. 'And my life. Now *you* get out too.'

'Me?' said Vlad. 'But I live here.'

'Not any more you don't,' yelled Dad, exploding. 'You get out – I've had enough.'

Then Dad grabbed a fly swot and began chasing Vlad with it.

'Get out of my house, I never want to see you again, you horrible vampire! Never, never, never, never!' he shouted as he tried to bash Vlad, who was always just a bit too quick for him.

The scene was one of total chaos as Mum came in through the front door, pushing past the publicity people who were filing out, loaded down with cameras and lights.

'It's like a madhouse,' she said. 'What on earth is going on?'

'Oh, Mum,' said Judy. 'Thank goodness

you've come home. Dad is chasing Vlad with a fly swot and trying to swot him!'

Dad came rushing downstairs in pursuit of Vlad, bashing the wall with the fly swot but always just missing.

'Swotting's too good for him,' yelled Dad. 'He's turned my house upside down.' And he raced after Vlad into the kitchen. Vlad flew up on to a shelf and jumped into a casserole dish. Mum followed them and grabbed Dad's arm.

'Nick, stop it! You'll break all my dishes!'

'Sorry love,' said Dad, 'but I can't stand it any more.'

'Calm down,' said Mum. 'You don't have to swot Vlad to get rid of him.'

'I know I don't *have* to,' said Dad, 'I just *want* to. I've been dreaming of this moment for weeks.'

'Now stop it!' Mum insisted. 'We've got to negotiate for Vlad to leave peaceably without wrecking the kitchen.'

Reluctantly Dad gave in and said that if Vlad came out and left the house that very evening he wouldn't be swotted.

'Vlad, do you hear?' called Mum. 'Dad won't try and swot you if you come out quietly.'

Vlad raised the lid of the casserole and hung out a white handkerchief.

'I surrender,' he called. 'I surrender unconditionally.'

So Vlad came out and went and sat in Judy's

room, while Mum and Judy packed up his things.

'I don't want to go,' complained Vlad. 'The Lord High is being very unreasonable. He went barmy, running round like a nut treating me as if I was a mosquito, when all I did was have a few people in for a bit of publicity. Can't you talk him round?'

'Doesn't look like it,' said Mum. 'You'll have to stay with Mal until you go back to Romania.'

'Poor old Vlad, poor little Drac,' moaned the vampire.

'And just think, Vlad,' said Judy, trying to cheer him up, 'you'll be able to say that whenever you want.'

'It's not nearly so much fun,' replied Vlad, 'when it doesn't annoy someone.'

9

Vlad Pays a Visit

So Vlad was bundled off to Malcolm Meilberg, who wasn't thrilled to see him.

The next day the Stones were having breakfast. Dad tucked into his with enthusiasm, Paul munched away, Mum picked at a piece of toast and Judy sat and looked miserable.

'Well, this is great,' said Dad. 'No Vlad – sanity at last! I've got my home back too – what a relief.'

'I miss him,' said Judy tearfully. 'I think you're being horrid.'

'Oh yes,' said Dad. 'Poor old Vlad, he's been treated so badly. We've been so unkind to him, after he was always so helpful and considerate.'

'Vlad's like that, Dad – he just does whatever he wants and doesn't think. I still think he's lovely,' said Judy defiantly.

'I agree with Dad,' said Paul. 'It's lovely without him. No one to call me Bunglethorpe and cause chaos – it's great!'

'He was a lot of trouble,' said Mum. 'You never knew what was going to happen next, but it was fun.'

'Fun?' exploded Dad. 'Fun? It was hell, and I don't want him in my house ever again. If you two want to see him off the premises that's fine.

but if I ever find him here, I'll take great pleasure in swotting him.'

Just then the phone rang.

'It's probably him,' said Dad. 'I'll take it.'

A moment later Dad came back. 'It's someone called Smee for you, Judy.'

So Judy went to the phone.

'Is that you, Judy?' squeaked a voice. 'It's me.'

'Oh hello, Vlad,' said Judy. 'Yes, I'm fine. Vlad, I'm sorry if you're miserable, I'm miserable too, but Dad won't have you back. No, not even for a visit. He says I can see you off the premises but you can't come here. No, you can't talk to him because he's just gone out.'

'Just stick around, kid,' said the vampire, 'and I'll be right over.'

'But, Vlad . . .' protested Judy, but it was too late. Vlad had hung up.

Judy went into the kitchen and whispered to Mum, 'It was Vlad, I didn't think and I told him Dad had gone out and so he's coming over.'

'Oh dear,' said Mum. 'We'd better get Paul out of the house, and as soon as Vlad arrives we'll pack him off back to Mal's.'

So Mum gave Paul a very long shopping list and told him not to use his bike as there would be too much shopping for him to carry safely. She gave him enough money to buy himself a hamburger and a milkshake too.

'That should keep him out of the way for a while.'

It took Vlad about half an hour to get to Willow

Road, and he flew from his car on to the window ledge and knocked on the window. Mum opened the window quickly

'Morning all,' said Vlad cheerfully. 'Can I come in?'

'Vlad, this is very naughty,' said Mum severely. 'You've got to go straight away. Dad and Paul are out, but if either of them should come back you're in dead trouble.'

'Why, what would they do?' asked Vlad.

'Well, Dad will certainly try to swot you,' explained Mum. 'So you've got to go straight away, and never come back.'

'It's not fair,' complained Vlad. 'I only feel at home in London when I'm here. That hotel of Mal's is too fancy. I don't feel comfortable in it.'

'It's entirely your own fault,' said Mum. 'You were warned and you took no notice, so go off quickly before Nick comes back.'

As she finished her sentence the front door banged. Mum and Judy looked at each other in panic.

'It's Dad!' cried Judy.

'Quick, Vlad,' said Mum, 'hide here in the flour bin.'

So Vlad dived into the flour bin. Dad came in to the kitchen, and opened all the windows.

'What are you doing, Nick?' asked Mum.

'I've just been out to buy lots and lots of garlic and I'm going to put it on the window sills. It's supposed to put vampires off.'

'Why are you doing that, Dad?' asked Judy. 'Do you think Vlad will try to pay us a visit?'

'I'm sure of it,' said Dad. 'That's why I'm doing this. I'm determined to get in first, so he'll never, never, never get into my home again.'

'Why don't you go and put the garlic out upstairs, darling,' suggested Mum.

'Are you trying to get rid of me?' said Dad suspiciously. 'Has anyone been here?'

'Nick, I can honestly tell you that the only people in this house are the three of us.'

'Umm,' said Dad. 'Well, let's keep it like that.' And he went upstairs.

Vlad climbed out of the flour bin and brushed himself down.

'He's a nut,' he told Mum. 'You're married to a nut.'

'No, I'm not!' said Mum. 'It's just that you have a bad effect on him. Now come on, let's get you out of here.'

'Just a minute,' said Vlad, and he nibbled a bit of the garlic Dad had put out. 'Mmm, delicious!'

'Come on!' snapped Mum. 'Quick, before it's too late.'

'Coming,' said Vlad, but just then they heard Dad coming downstairs. Vlad made a dive for the cocoa jar as Dad came in.

'You two don't seem to be doing much this morning,' he commented, washing his hands at the sink to get the garlic smell off. 'Why are you hanging round the kitchen? Are you expecting someone?'

'No, Dad,' said Judy. 'We're not expecting anyone who isn't here.'

'Good,' said Dad, 'because if you were, I'd swot them the moment they walked in the door.'

'Would you like a cup of tea or coffee, dear?' asked Mum.

'No,' said Dad, 'I think I'll make myself a cup of cocoa.'

'Oh no,' said Judy. 'Let me make it for you, Dad. You've been having a really hard time lately – you've been doing far too much.'

So Judy made the cocoa, making great efforts to avoid Vlad as she took out the spoonfuls of powder.

Dad drank his cocoa. 'That's better,' he said. 'Well, I shall now resume normal living, I shall go and practise my violin, and enjoy the peace and quiet of my own home.'

Vlad peeped out of the tin. 'Has the Lord High gone?' he asked as he climbed out and brushed the brown cocoa off himself.

'You really must go,' said Mum. 'Not another moment to be wasted – you climb out of the window and down the drainpipe and hide in the garden. Judy will go and get her bike and then she'll come round and pick you up and take you to your car.'

'It's waiting round the corner,' whispered Vlad. 'I didn't want the Lord High to see it.'

'Go on,' said Mum. 'Not another word.'

So Vlad slipped out of the window, down the pipe and hid among the plants. Judy rode up on her bike and was just about to pick Vlad up when Dad came out into the garden with the lawnmower.

'I thought you were going to practise, Dad,' said Judy.

'I was,' said Dad, 'but I'm still too angry. I'm going to mow the lawn for a bit. That should make me feel better.'

So Vlad cowered among the plants while Dad pushed the lawnmower along.

'Every time this machine gobbles up a dandelion, I pretend it's Vlad,' Dad told Judy. 'And when I've finished mowing, I'm going to weed all the flower beds and imagine all the weeds I pull up by the roots are Vlad.'

'I'll help, Dad,' said Judy. 'Let me do the weeding, and then I'll put the weeds in the basket on my bike and take them to the people down the road who've got a compost heap.'

'You don't usually help in the garden,' said Dad.

'I'm bored,' Judy replied, 'with Vlad gone. I'll weed this bed over here under the window. Just look at all these weeds, It can't have been done for ages.' And Judy picked up a pile of weeds and Vlad along with them, and dumped them all in her basket.

'I'll just take these weeds down the road,' she said.

'Hang on,' said Dad. 'Not so fast. Let's finish weeding the whole garden and then you can take all the weeds away at once.'

So Vlad sat in Judy's basket while the weeds were piled in on top of him. They had nearly finished and Judy was about to ride off, when Paul came back with the shopping.

'Hi, Dad!' said Paul. 'You know, it's an odd thing but I'm sure I saw Vlad's car parked round the corner.'

'I knew it!' yelled Dad. 'I knew it, I knew he was around here somewhere. Well he won't get in. I've put garlic on all the window sills and we'll go in and lock the doors and we won't answer the door no matter how many times he rings. We'll take the phone off the hook and light fires in every room, so he can't fly down the chimney!'

'But Dad,' said Paul, 'it's the middle of summer.'

'I don't care,' said Dad. 'I just want to keep that vampire off my premises. Judy, you go and deliver the compost and then come straight back because in ten minutes the doors are going to be locked for the whole day.'

'Where are you taking the compost?' asked Paul.

'To those people up the road who have a big compost heap,' said Judy.

'I don't know of anyone with a compost heap,' replied Paul.

'Well, there are lots of things you don't know,' said Judy getting on her bike. 'Back in a minute or two,' and she cycled off.

When she had cycled out of Dad and Paul's view she stopped and breathed a sigh of relief and tried to dig Vlad out. Vlad surfaced, pushing the weeds aside and wiping the mud off his face.

'It's an outrage,' he complained. '*Me* having to hide in flour bins and cocoa jars and under weeds. The indignity of it all. The Lord High is being very difficult. I shan't visit again until he calms down and behaves more like a normal human being, assuming there is any such thing as a *normal* human being. Take me to my car, Flunglebunge. I don't hold this barbaric behaviour against you or Mum – you're not bad as people go – but as for the Lord High and Bunglethorpe, I am at a loss for words.'

So Judy took Vlad to the waiting car.

'I can't bear to see you go like this,' said Judy sniffing and trying not to cry. 'I don't like to think of you being in London and not living with us.'

'Just try not to think about it, my little Flunglebunge,' said Vlad. 'Maybe one day you and Mum can come and stay with us in Romania, and I promise neither Mrs Vlad nor I will try to swot you, no matter what the provocation. Of course, I couldn't answer for young Ghitza. I never know what that naughty little vampire will be up to next.'

'I'll miss you, Vlad,' said Judy.

'I'll miss you too,' said Vlad. 'But the Lord High has come between us, so I'm afraid there's no future in this relationship. I'll find a way to say goodbye to you and Mum before I leave.' And Vlad flew into his car and it drove away, leaving a tearful Judy looking after him.

10

For He's a Jolly Good Vampire

For a few days the Stones heard nothing of Vlad, and Dad was convinced that the vampire had gone out of their lives for ever and he began to relax.

Judy went on missing Vlad, but after a while she began playing with Paul as usual. But one afternoon they were out cycling together when a huge truck suddenly swerved towards them and hit Paul's bike. He was sent flying over the handlebars into a tree. He lay on the ground unconscious, his head bleeding. Judy knelt next to him not knowing what to do. Someone rang for an ambulance and took Judy home to tell her parents. As soon as Judy had told Dad what had happened, he phoned Mum at her surgery and then went straight to the hospital with Judy. Mum came over as soon as she could.

Later that evening the Stones sat round Paul's bed, gazing at the still figure and white face. Suddenly Dad remembered that he'd arranged to meet Malcolm Meilberg for a drink and went off to find a phone and cancel the arrangement. He came back to Paul's bed, which was in a little room off the main ward.

'Malcolm was very upset to hear what had

happened and he's coming over to give us support.' he told them quietly.

A little later Malcolm Meilberg arrived. He crept into the room where Paul was.

'How is he?' he asked.

'He's still unconscious,' said Mum, trying not to cry.

'Oh dear,' said Malcolm Meilberg. 'What a sad sight, poor kid. Look Nick, I hope you don't mind but Vlad was with me when you phoned and when he heard the news he was terribly upset. He insists that he feels he's one of the family and that he ought to be with you at this time. I had to bring him with me, he's waiting outside. Can I bring him in?'

'Of course,' said Dad. 'Vlad's sins don't seem very important compared to this, and I suppose he *is* one of the family really.'

So Malcolm Meilberg went and fetched Vlad, who sat on the end of Paul's bed and looked at the still figure swathed in bandages.

'Oh poor Bunglethorpe,' he said, tears running down his face. 'When will he wake up?'

'We don't know,' sighed Mum.

'You all look exhausted,' said Vlad. 'I think you should all go home and have some sleep and leave me to keep an eye on poor old Bunglethorpe.'

'What about you, Vlad?' asked Mum. 'Don't you need sleep?'

'We vampires are creatures of the night,' Vlad informed her. 'While people sleep, the vampires roam. You get some sleep and don't worry about me, you've got enough to worry about.'

'I think Vlad's right, love,' said Dad. 'You're exhausted. You and Judy go home and Vlad and I will keep watch and tell you if anything happens.'

'Well alright. I suppose it would be best,' said Mum. 'Thanks, Vlad. It's nice to have you back.'

'Oh, Vlad,' wept Judy, 'I'm so worried about Paul.'

'Don't worry, Flunglebunge,' said Vlad, flying on to her shoulder. 'You go home and get some sleep, and by tomorrow he'll have come round, you'll see.'

'I'll drive you two ladies home,' said Malcolm Meilberg. 'We'll leave Dad and Vlad to their vigil. Let me know if anything happens. It doesn't matter how late it is, I want to know, right?'

'Right,' said Dad.

'Right,' said Vlad.

'Glad you're here, Vlad,' said Mum, 'even though it is in such sad circumstances.' Then the three of them went home, leaving Dad and Vlad sitting with Paul.

'Hope you don't mind me being here,' said Vlad.

'To be honest,' replied Dad, 'I'm pleased to see you. When the chips are down, you really are one of the family.'

'Sorry about all the trouble I caused,' said Vlad. 'I've been thinking about it over the last few days, and I have been very bad. Don't blame you for wanting to swot me.'

'It's alright,' said Dad. 'I promise I'll never try to swot you again.'

'Shake,' said Vlad. So Dad held out his hand and Vlad took it.

'Listen, Lord High,' said Vlad. 'Why don't you get a bit of kip and I'll wake you up if anything happens.'

So Dad dozed off and Vlad sat on the end bed post and didn't take his eyes off Paul for a second. In the middle of the night, Paul stirred and muttered and opened his eyes for a moment. Vlad beamed with joy.

'Hello, Bunglethorpe,' he whispered quietly.

'Watcha, Boris,' muttered Paul, and he smiled and went back to sleep. Vlad did a head over heels and then woke Dad.

'Bunglethorpe's going to be alright, he woke up and he called me Boris. Do you hear me? Bunglethorpe is going to be alright. Woopee,' and before Dad could stop him Vlad flew off.

Vlad sailed off through the darkened wards of the hospital calling out to the sleeping patients, 'It's alright, you don't have to worry, Bunglethorpe's going to be alright, he called me Boris!' Then, flying on his back through the next ward, he shouted out, 'Bunglethorpe called me Boris. Hurray!'

Vlad flew on, through ward after ward, waking everyone up until eventually a Night Sister managed to catch him.

'Now what is going on?' she demanded. 'Why are you waking up all the patients?'

'Because they must all want to know that Bunglethorpe is going to get better.'

'All those people are very ill,' said the Sister severely, 'and they need their sleep.'

'All those people are ill?' said Vlad, horrified. 'Oh dear, I didn't realize.'

'This is a hospital,' said the Sister, 'so it's full of ill people.'

'Oh, I see,' said Vlad. 'All sick like poor Bunglethorpe?'

'That's right, so you stop making all that noise.'

'I'll be very, very quiet,' whispered Vlad.

'Good,' said the Sister. 'Come on, we'll go and sit in my office and you can tell me all about your friend Bun-what's-his-name?'

'Bunglethorpe,' whispered Vlad, following the Sister into her office. 'He called me Boris.'

Vlad and the Sister sat down and had a chat. She told him all about her family in the West Indies and he told her all about the Stones and Malcolm Meilberg and Mrs Vlad and his five children. They were deeply involved in the conversation when a light went on and there in the doorway were five hospital porters and six doctors, two carrying butterfly nets.

'Hello,' whispered Vlad. 'Don't make a sound, all the people are ill.'

At that moment a net came down on Vlad.

'Got him!' said a doctor.

'Let me out!' said Vlad wriggling. 'I didn't do anything, why am I in here?'

'You've been waking up the whole hospital, everyone's complaining.'

'I only told them that Bunglethorpe had called me Boris. I didn't know they were ill and that they didn't know Bunglethorpe. I didn't mean to wake them up.'

'It's alright, Doctor,' said the Sister. 'He got a bit over-excited because his friend what's-his-name is recovering. I've explained the situation, he won't do it again.'

'Well, alright,' said the doctor dubiously, and he released Vlad from his imprisonment.

'Now, no more shouting,' he said strictly, 'or back you go.'

So Vlad went back to Paul's bedside and sat there till dawn. In the morning the doctors said Paul would have to stay in hospital for a few days.

'I'll come and see you every day, Bunglethorpe, and you'll never get bored.'

'Every day,' groaned Paul. 'I want to go home!'

Paul was taken into the main ward and Vlad kept his word and turned up every day. He rapidly became a great favourite in the ward and he flew from bed to bed, talking to everyone, telling them about his Great Uncle Ghitza and threatening to vampirise anyone who didn't take their medicine. On one occasion he even practised unwinding a bandage. At visiting time Vlad noticed there was one little boy who never got any visitors and so Vlad always went to talk to him.

'Me name's Kevin,' said the boy. 'I'm one of seven kids. Me mum can't come to see me 'cos

there's no one to look after the others and me dad works overtime.'

'Oh dear,' said Vlad, 'I wouldn't like it one bit if one of my little vampires was ill and Mrs Vlad, I mean Magda and I couldn't visit them. I know, I'll go and look after the children every day, so your mum and dad can visit.'

So every day Vlad took his car to Kevin's house and sent his mum to the hospital in it. He played with the children and gave them tea, and told them if anyone misbehaved they'd get vampirized. Then when the car came back, Vlad would return to the hospital. It all worked out very well and Kevin started to get better.

'Mum says the kids are having a smashing time with you,' said Kevin. 'Will you come and visit us when I go home?'

''Course,' agreed Vlad. 'But you'll have to get well fast, as I'm going home to Romania soon.'

At first the doctors and nurses had been a bit worried about the effect of having a vampire in the ward, but Vlad proved a useful ally and the doctor in charge of the ward told him, 'You've done a good job. It's been a much happier ward since you've been here.'

Vlad glowed with pride. 'It's nothing,' he informed the doctor. 'Being a father of five, I have a way with children. Vampires and children get on fine anyway.'

The day before Paul left to go home, all the staff in the hospital decided to give Vlad a party. A big cake was made but it was decided to keep it a secret. Vlad was doing his usual rounds when the cake was wheeled in. It was three layers and had writing on it in pink, saying, 'Well done, Boris the Bat.'

'A cake for me!' exclaimed Vlad. 'But why? It's not my birthday, it's not my official or my unofficial birthday.'

'Well,' said Dad, 'since you've been so good and kind to everyone in this ward, we decided it was your semi-official birthday and thought we'd hold a party for you.'

'Oh!' said Vlad. 'How wonderful. I don't know what to say.'

'That makes a change,' said Paul.

'I think you're getting better, Bunglethorpe,' said Vlad.

'Certainly am,' agreed Paul. 'Oh Vlad, I've been asked to present you with this gift and this card as a token of appreciation for everything you've done in the last few days, and to help you remember us when you go back to Romania.'

Vlad first of all opened the card. 'What a lot of people have signed it. It says, "To Boris the Bat from the Lord High, Grottberger, Flunglebunge, Bunglethorpe, the Abominable, Podsnap, Snodgrass and Slugberry, Mum and Kevin and all the staff and patients in the children's ward." Oh, aren't you all nice. Mrs Vlad will be pleased when she sees this.

'Now for the present, what can it be?' – Vlad pulled the paper open and then opened the box and there inside was a Vlad-sized bicycle. Vlad leapt on it and cycled round and round his cake.

Dad grabbed him. 'Alright, Vlad, you can take it home. But first you must take a piece of cake to all your fans.'

So Vlad flew around the ward taking cake to everyone. When he'd finished, everyone started to sing,

'For he's a jolly good vampire,
For he's a jolly good vampire,
For he's a jolly good vampire,
Which no one (not even Dad) can deny.
Which nobody can deny,
Which nobody can deny,
For he's a jolly good vampire,
For he's a jolly good vampire,
For he's a jolly good vampire,
And so say all of us.'

Vlad jumped up and down with delight, and leapt on his bike and rode round and round in circles. He blew kisses as he went and yelled, 'Thank you, thank you all, I love you all.'

'Come on, Vlad,' said Dad. 'Off your bike. Come and say thank you properly.'

So Vlad got off his bike and stood on the bottom layer of the cake:

'Ladies and gentlemen I want to thank you for your good wishes, your lovely presents and above all for calling me a "Jolly Good Vampire", and I want to say I think all you people are lovely too and I'm not going to vampirise any of you, not

Bunglethorpe, nor the Lord High, nor Slugberry nor Flunglebunge nor even the Abominable, because you're all jolly good people! Rumbumbelow! Good old Vlad! Lucky little Drac!'

Lucy and the Big Bad Wolf by Ann Jungman

When Lucy Jones goes to visit her grandparents wearing her new red anorak, she has no idea she will meet the Big Bad Wolf. The wolf follows her to London, where he soon finds himself thoroughly out of his depth – and Lucy finds herself involved in lots of amazing adventures.

Lucy and the Wolf in Sheep's Clothing by Ann Jungman

The wolf returns to London to look up his old friends, and rapidly becomes the most wanted wolf in the city. As the police search for him, he tries to find a foolproof disguise, with hilarious results. And when a businessman called Sir Samuel Wolf is kidnapped – well, we can all guess who's behind it!

Lucy Keeps the Wolf from the Door by Ann Jungman

When the wolf becomes the proud father of three little wolf cubs, things change: the granny-muncher of the fairy tale is gone, replaced by a vegetarian campaigner against acid rain. But *some* things never change, and the wolf's talent for causing chaos is one of them...

All at £2.99.

All these books are available at your local bookshop or newsagent, or can be ordered from the publishers.

To order direct from the publishers just tick the titles you want and fill in the form below:

Name ____

Address ____

____

Send to: Collins Children's Cash Sales
PO Box 11
Falmouth
Cornwall
TR10 9EN

Please enclose a cheque or postal order or debit my Visa/Access –

Credit card no:

Expiry date:

Signature:

– to the value of the cover price plus:

UK: 80p for the first book, and 20p per copy for each additional book ordered to a maximum charge of £2.00.

BFPO: 80p for the first book, and 20p per copy for each additional book.

Overseas and Eire: £1.50 for the first book, £1.00 for the second book, thereafter 30p per book.

Young Lions reserve the right to show new retail prices on covers which may differ from those previously advertised in the text or elsewhere.

Young Lions